THE DARK CLIFFS

From the author of 633 Squadron...

Soon after Kate Fielding arrived at Whitesands, a dark and brooding house on the Cornish cliffs, she found herself threatened by a secret from the past. Why had Philip Leavengate's wife fallen to her death last year? What connection had the dead woman's cousin with the sinister house-keeper, Mrs Treher. Why were both of them so frightened of a seemingly innocent young boy who came visiting at Whitesands? Determined to unravel the shadowy mystery, Kate found her new love – and her life itself – in deadly peril. An unknown, unseen force of evil began filling her days with horror, and her nights with unspeakable terror.

THE DARK CLIFFS

THE DARK CLIFFS

by

Frederick E. Smith

Dales Large Print Books
Long Preston, North Yorkshire,
BD23 4ND, England.

British Library Cataloguing in Publication Data.

Smith, Frederick E.
    The dark cliffs.

    A catalogue record of this book is
    available from the British Library

    ISBN   978-1-84262-558-3 pbk

Originally published in 1962 under the title The Other Cousin

Published in Large Print 2008 by arrangement with
Frederick E. Smith

Dales Large Print is an imprint of Library Magna Books Ltd.

Printed and bound in Great Britain by
T.J. (International) Ltd., Cornwall, PL28 8RW

1

'Kate!' The child's shrill voice was full of excitement. 'Kate – Aunt Caroline's coming!'

In the nursery Kate Fielding stiffened over the bed she was making. She heard Sarah's footsteps enter the long corridor and scamper down it. 'Kate, isn't it exciting? Kate, where are you...?'

'I'm here,' Kate called. 'In your room.'

Sarah, a pretty eleven-year-old child with an oval face and bobbing chestnut hair, burst excitedly into the room. 'Did you hear me, Kate? Aunt Caroline's coming. Daddy's just had a telegram. Isn't it splendid?'

Kate managed a smile. 'Yes, dear. When does she arrive?'

'Sometime today. Daddy says the telegram was sent from Exeter. So she could be here in a few hours.'

A few hours, Kate thought. It was all so characteristic of everything she had heard of Caroline. A spontaneous decision by an exciting personality, followed by immediate action. One moment in Italy or France, the next in England and on her way to Whitesands. Only was it quite as spontaneous as that? a small doubting voice inside her asked...

Sarah's inquisitive voice pulled her together. 'What's the matter, Kate? Why are you looking like that?'

Kate turned hastily back to the bed. 'Nothing, dear. Just thinking thoughts, that's all.' As she tucked in the blankets she glanced back over her shoulder. 'How long is your aunt going to stay? Did your father say?'

'No, the telegram just said she was on her way.' Sarah's voice was suddenly anxious. 'But she wouldn't come all this way for a day or two, would she?'

'I shouldn't think so,' Kate comforted. She smoothed down the coverlet and then turned to Sarah with a smile. 'You like Aunt Caroline, don't you?'

Sarah was all enthusiasm again. 'Oh, yes, Kate; she's fun. You ought to see her dresses – they're simply gorgeous. And she has the most wonderful perfumes and things...' It was obvious from Sarah's starry-eyed face that she was a willing victim of Caroline's glamour. 'She has an emerald brooch that an Italian count gave her. And she's met film stars and all kinds of people over there.'

'She does sound exciting.' Kate smiled. She hesitated, then went on: 'Does Mrs Treherne like her too?'

Sarah's flushed face clouded in sudden dislike. 'I don't know but I shouldn't think so. She doesn't like anybody, does she?'

Kate had the sudden desire to ask the child how much her father, Philip Leavengate, liked Caroline but remembered herself in time. Always, whenever Philip came into her mind, her thoughts had a way of disintegrating and confusing her. 'Where's John?' she asked instead, finding safety in the question.

'He was playing on the front lawn with his tricycle when I left him.' At this reminder of more mundane things than Caroline, Sarah remembered her own affairs. 'Can I go down to the beach this morning, Kate? Mary and Betty want me to play with them.'

Kate nodded. 'Yes, but only if you promise not to go near the sea. You've only to go swimming when one of us is with you.'

'I promise. Thanks, Kate.' At the door Sarah swung round. 'Oh; I've just remembered. Daddy wants you to see him before you go into town this morning. He's got some papers he wants you to take to his office.'

'I won't forget. You run along now but be careful.'

'Thanks, Kate. Bye-bye...'

As Sarah skipped happily down the corridor Kate turned slowly to the window that overlooked the north Cornish cliffs. Ever since she had heard of Caroline Worth, the cousin of Philip's deceased wife, Elizabeth, it had seemed inevitable she must come sooner or later to Whitesands. And now it was to happen what need would Philip have for a children's nurse with another young and capable woman in the house?

The thought of leaving Whitesands made Kate close her eyes for a moment. Five and a half months ago, when she had applied for the post, it had seemed nothing more than a chance to escape for a while from the smoke and turmoil of London. Only a small chance too, because at twenty-six she had believed herself too young for the post. Standing there by the window she remembered her interview with Philip Leavengate as if it had happened yesterday. She had been expecting to meet a middle-aged man – instead the man at the desk had been in his thirties, tall, dark-haired, with blue-grey eyes that had seemed both penetrating and sad. Although very sombrely dressed in a black suit, he had appeared quite relaxed, until her training made her notice the pallor of his face and the tiny grief-lines around his mouth. As he offered her a chair she had found herself wondering what secret sorrow he was bearing.

Yet for a moment the lines had vanished as his firm mouth had quirked humorously. 'You know, Miss Fielding, I had really intended employing someone considerably older than yourself. Yet according to my agent you have more qualifications than any of the other applicants. I understand you've had nursing experience with children?'

'Yes. I'm a State Registered nurse and worked for two years in the Sandown Children's Hospital.'

'And according to these notes you've had business experience as well.'

'Yes. I've been the personal secretary to a business director for another two years.'

'Why did you give up nursing for business?'

She had liked him for asking the question. 'My father didn't leave much money when he died. I've a younger sister and a very young brother, and when I found I couldn't help my mother sufficiently I took the secretarial post. I really had no choice – it was so much better paid.'

He had nodded understandingly. 'I see. And I believe you like children.'

'Oh, yes. Very much.'

'And how do they get on with you?'

'Rather well, I think. At least I always found that in the hospital.'

His eyes had crinkled warmly at her, making her think how much younger he looked when he smiled. In the brief silence that followed she noticed his hands. They were clean-looking, slightly tanned with sinewy fingers and well-kept nails. Eyes and hands had always been the two things she had noticed about men. As her gaze lifted she saw the grief-lines had returned to his face.

'My wife was killed in an accident just over two weeks ago, Miss Fielding, leaving two children, Sarah who is eleven and John, a little chap of four. As my wife had been ill for some months prior to her accident we had a nurse looking after them, but she had to leave last week for personal reasons – I understand she is going to join her brother in Canada – and I want someone to take her place. I don't think it is a very difficult job: Sarah is hardly any trouble now and John is quite a good little chap. And, of course, I have a woman, Mrs Treherne, who does all the housework and the cooking.'

It was only now that Kate had realised he was in mourning – the agent had made no mention of such a recent bereavement – and she had felt embarrassment as she murmured her condolences. He had nodded and interrupted her before she could finish, not with curtness but with an urgency that came from grief.

'You might be wondering why I also asked for someone with a little business experience. The estate at Whitesands is fairly large and my practice – I'm a solicitor in St Marks – doesn't give me all the time I'd like to attend to it. Until she became too ill my wife used to handle the less complicated matters, such as paying the staff their wages, handling their insurance cards, income tax, and so on, and if you have the time perhaps you could take these things from me.' His smile had been very reassuring. 'If you think you'd like to give the job a trial I think I can promise not to overload you.'

And so Kate had come to Cornwall. Whitesands was a large house, built of grey stone so that it looked as if it had grown from the massive cliffs around it. It stood on the curve of a small bay, facing the cliffs which were perhaps a quarter of a mile away. The estate, which was contained between the cliffs and the main road to St Marks, consisted mostly of stone-hedged fields, and after being used to the lusher countryside around London, Kate's first impression had been one of bleakness. There were no high green hedges here and few trees to soften the view; the eye could sweep unchecked to the distant, cloud-shadowed moors. She had learned from Philip, who had fetched her himself from the station, that the estate included the small beach enclosed by the bay.

'The house is called Whitesands because the sand on our beach is the whitest you ever saw,' he told her.

There were three permanent servants at Whitesands when Kate arrived: a farm manager called Marsden, a gardener and handyman called Wirral who helped Marsden in his spare time, and Mrs Treherne. Mrs Treherne, although an excellent cook and

13

efficient housekeeper, was a withdrawn, dark-visaged woman whom it was difficult to get to know, she being dour to the point of rudeness. The children disliked her, and sometimes Kate felt their dislike was akin to fear, for neither was happy if left alone with her. She had been at Whitesands for over a year, being the replacement of old Margot the previous housekeeper who had been forced to retire through old age. It was some time before Kate learned it had not been Philip who had discovered Mrs Treherne but Caroline Worth, his dead wife's cousin.

In the weeks that followed Kate was to hear a great deal about the glamorous Caroline, mostly from the chatter of Sarah to whom Caroline was a most exciting personality. Caroline whose address could be Cannes one day and Rome the next... Caroline of the beautiful clothes ... the expensive gifts. Caroline whose unexpected visits brought an exciting breath of the Continent to Whitesands...

From the chance remarks Kate heard from other members of the household, some from Philip himself, she gained a somewhat different mental picture of Caroline from the one Sarah held. Under the façade of glamour Caroline seemed an efficient, capable woman, and the feeling had grown on Kate that her arrival at Whitesands, if prolonged, could mean nothing less than her own eventual redundancy.

It was a thought that was to become leavened by emotion as the months passed by. For Kate had soon discovered that Philip's grief at his wife's death went much deeper than his outward appearance suggested, and in the difficult weeks that followed she had quietly sympathised and helped him in every way she could. She had felt his appreciation, and although both had preserved the formalities of their positions, the outcome was they had become more like friends than employer and employee. What this might one day signify Kate had never allowed herself to consider. All she would admit was that Whitesands, with the two motherless children who had taken her to their hearts and whom she had grown to love, had became a dearly-precious chapter in her life, and the very thought that Caroline's arrival might bring it to a close was enough to bring her pain.

She turned away from the window, a slim girl of average height with a boyish crop of dark hair and a sensitive, attractive face. As she descended the long, curved staircase she heard the faint click-click of a typewriter coming from a door on the left of the hall. Hesitating a moment she knocked on it and entered.

Philip glanced up from his desk, his eyes clearing on recognising her. As she approached him she saw again the glint of silver in the dark hair around his temples, something that had barely been noticeable five and a half months ago. The rush of tenderness that the thought evoked made her voice slightly self-conscious.

'Sarah tells me you want me to deliver some papers to your office this morning.'

He nodded, reaching out for a large, bulky envelope. 'If you wouldn't mind, Kate. Ask Redfearn to witness them and get them off in today's post, will you – I want them to arrive first thing on Monday morning. You'll take the car, of course.'

She took the envelope and the car keys from him. 'Thank you. I'll see he gets them in good time.'

As she was turning for the door his voice checked her. 'You've heard the news, haven't you – that Elizabeth's cousin is coming?'

She turned back slowly. 'Yes. Sarah mentioned it a few minutes ago.'

He laughed. 'I could hear the little beggar shouting it out from here. She's got quite a crush on her Aunt Caroline.'

'Is it true that she might arrive very soon?'

'It looks like it. Her telegram was sent from Exeter and said she was "on her way". If she's still driving around in expensive sports cars it oughtn't to take her long.' There was humour on Philip's lean face. 'Sudden surprises like this are typical of Carol, I'm afraid.'

Carol... Kate felt shame at her pang of jealousy.

'What about a room for her? Have you spoken to Mrs Treherne?'

'Yes. She's getting the sun room ready. We may as well use it as leave it empty.'

After Elizabeth's bedroom, which was still closed, the sun room was the most attractive room upstairs, with large French windows and a deep balcony. Elizabeth herself had used it as a sitting-room before becoming a chronic invalid... Kate felt the dull ache inside her spread and told herself she was behaving like a schoolgirl. 'Did Miss Worth say how long she is coming for?' she asked.

'No. But not very long, I shouldn't think. If I know Carol, the wanderlust will soon catch up with her again.'

But do you know Carol, Kate thought. She heard her voice again, reassuringly businesslike now. 'Is there anything I can do to help Mrs Treherne?'

'No. I've told Wirral to give her a hand with the furniture – between them they'll manage easily enough. You go into town and do your shopping.' His blue-grey eyes were searching her face. 'You've been looking a little pale recently. You should take more time off.'

She felt her cheeks colouring under his concern. 'There's nothing wrong with me.'

He shook his head warmly. 'You haven't spared yourself these last few months, Kate.

That's one reason I'm quite glad Caroline is coming. The children like her and she's efficient around the house – it'll give you a chance to take a holiday.'

Her protest spilled out before she could contain it. 'But I don't want a holiday. Why should I want one?' As his eyebrows lifted in quizzical surprise she moved awkwardly towards the door. 'I don't want one this year – really I don't … I'd better be getting along to town now. If you want Sarah she's down on the beach playing with Mary and Betty. I reminded her not to go near the sea. John is playing with his tricycle on the front lawn.'

'Mrs Treherne knows you're going, doesn't she?'

'Oh, yes. And I've asked her to keep her eye on John.'

'Then off you go and don't worry. You don't need to hurry back – take your time and enjoy yourself.'

Outside his study door she paused, still conscious of the heat in her cheeks. Then she turned and went back upstairs. The sun room was in the opposite wing of Whitesands to her own bedroom. She went to it and paused in the open doorway.

Wirral, the gardener and handyman, was busy assembling the mirror to a dressing-table that had been dragged into the room. He was a man in his late fifties with stringy limbs and a weatherbeaten, wrinkled face.

At some affray in the past his nose had been broken, and its permanent slant, coupled to a pair of eyebrows as shaggy as a Scots terrier, gave him an expression that was both fierce and woebegone. Seeing Kate in the doorway he wrinkled his forehead comically at Mrs Treherne's back – he and the housekeeper were mortal enemies.

Mrs Treherne was halfway up a pair of steps, hanging a new set of curtains across the big bay window. As she reached up to the curtain rail her lifting dress revealed a pair of muscular calves. She was a thick-set, powerful woman with skin dark enough to have belonged to a southern Spaniard. Kate was certain the woman knew she was in the doorway, but she gave no sign of it.

'Mrs Treherne, I'm going now. Is there anything I can get you in St Marks?'

At that the housekeeper turned her head. She had the face of a peasant, square and strong with watchful eyes that were like beads of jet. Her dour expression did not change as she stared at Kate. 'No, miss. I've got everything I want this week.'

She turned back to the curtains. Feeling she might be resenting the extra work put on her Kate went on: 'I've heard that Miss Worth is coming today. Can I do anything to help you before I go?'

This time Mrs Treherne did not bother to turn her head. 'No, thank you, miss. We can manage quite well.'

Kate turned to Wirral, who grimaced his dislike at the housekeeper's broad back. 'Is there anything I can get you, Mr Wirral?' she asked, trying to hide her rueful smile.

Wirral had a slightly plaintive voice with the huskiness of the heavy cigarette smoker. 'I don't think so, thanks, miss. I was in St Marks myself a couple o' days back.'

Kate left the two of them in their silent hostility and went outside for the car. It was standing in front of the garage and she realised with pleasure that Philip must have driven it out for her before giving her the keys. It was a large, powerful saloon – although unostentatious with his money in all other things Philip had a weakness for cars, and he had bought this one since Kate had arrived at Whitesands.

She started up the powerful engine and drove round to the front of the house. John, a solemn, pixie-faced child, was doing figure-eights on his tricycle on the closely-cropped lawn. He saw her, jumped off the tricycle and came running towards her. She stopped the car and wound down the opposite window.

'Be a good boy and stay near the house while I'm away.'

He nodded. He had a faint, attractive lisp. 'Where's daddy, Kate?'

'He's in his study. And Mrs Treherne is in

the big sun room upstairs if you want her. Stay near the house and I'll bring you a surprise back from St Marks.'

His solemn face brightened. 'What sort of surprise?'

'You wait and see,' she laughed. 'Bye-bye.'

He waved to her as she pulled away. To reach the main road to St Marks she had to drive west along the cliffs for nearly a mile and then turn left at a small hamlet. A few minutes more and she was passing Whitesands again, now diminished by distance. It was a fine June morning, and staring across the stone-hedged fields of the estate Kate was reminded how barren she had thought them when she first arrived. Now she had grown to love the cloud-shadowed countryside with its bold horizons and she knew she would feel imprisoned in London if forced to return there.

As if to emphasise the thought the stone hedges suddenly fell away as the road dipped and high impenetrable bushes, rising sheer from the road sides, took their place. It was a dank, dark stretch of road, with overhanging trees keeping out the sunlight, and she felt relief when the car climbed from it and topped a shallow hill. From it she could see the stone houses of St Marks five miles away and a few minutes later she was threading the car through its narrow streets to Philip's offices.

Dereck Redfearn, Philip's junior partner, was perhaps six years younger than Philip, a lanky young man with a racy turn of conversation and an eye for the girls, as Kate had already discovered. Not at all the type of person one generally associated with his profession. When she had once made this comment to Philip he had laughed. 'Professions don't really have types like that, Kate – at least I hope not. Don't let Dereck's lighthearted manner deceive you. He's really a first-class solicitor.'

Good solicitor or not Dereck was clearly delighted to see Kate as she was shown into his office. 'I don't believe it! You're a ghost – a figment of my desire.'

'I'm anything but a figment or whatever you call it,' she said, thrusting the thick envelope at him. 'Here's some work for you. Mr Leavengate says he wants the documents witnessing and sending off in today's post.'

He made a wry face at her. 'I thought for a moment you'd come to recant.'

'To recant what?'

'Your cruel refusal to go driving with me on one of these fine summer evenings.'

'I thought you had a new blonde who was occupying your spare time. One with lots of money.'

He grinned. 'You mean Sandra? The trouble there is that her father thinks I'm after her lolly. How suspicious can people be?'

He would not be past it, she knew. There was a ruthless, ambitious streak in him that had escaped Philip.

'You'll probably win him over with that fatal charm,' she said. 'Now I must be going – I've shopping to do.'

He jumped to his feet. 'Wait a minute. You've only just arrived. Come and have coffee with me. I haven't an appointment before eleven.'

She hesitated. 'What about the documents? Shouldn't you be seeing to them straight away?'

He took hold of her arm. 'Don't worry your pretty head about documents. There's plenty of time. Come on – it's weeks since I saw you.'

He led her across the narrow street to a quaint old café with leaded windows and a timbered roof. Stretching out his long legs he grinned at her across the table. 'Well – what's new since I saw you last?'

The temptation had been with her ever since she had walked into his office and this proved too much. 'Dereck, what's Caroline really like? You have met her, haven't you?'

He stared at her. 'You mean Caroline Worth? Elizabeth's cousin?'

'Yes. What's she like?'

He rounded his eyes in mock relish. 'Mm-mmm. Very, very glamorous indeed. Nice and Cannes from her high heels to her blonde hair-do. But what brings her to your mind on this fair sunny morning?'

She told him. He showed no surprise. 'The only mystery to me is why she hasn't come sooner.'

'Why do you say that?' she asked.

'Come off it, darling. Women usually jump on these things quicker than men.'

Her throat was dry now as she realised she was going to hear more than she feared. 'What things? What are you talking about?'

'Surely you must have heard how both she and Elizabeth were involved with Philip before he got married?'

'How could I hear a thing like that? I'm only a servant at Whitesands.'

She knew he had guessed her affection for Philip. It showed now in the tiny glint of malice in his eyes. 'A very faithful servant, too, darling. Phil's a lucky man.' As she coloured in embarrassment he went on: 'The story goes that thirteen years ago it was Caroline who met Philip first. What she was after I don't know – perhaps Whitesands and his position, perhaps the dear boy himself – anyway she had quite a crush on him. Feeling confident in herself, I suppose, she didn't bother to keep him from meeting Elizabeth, and that was a mistake. Because apparently Elizabeth was quite a stunner in those days – a better-looker than Caroline herself – and naughty old Philip "transferred his affections" as they say in the Sunday newspapers. Since then Caroline has been living it up on the Continent apart for the odd occasion when she's nipped over to cast a maternal eye on the lovers.'

Kate had a feeling of numbness as she listened to him.

'With these facts to chew on, you can make as good a guess as mine why she's coming. Mine is that she's going to make certain the fish doesn't get away the second time.'

Out of loyalty to Philip Kate had to protest. 'You oughtn't to talk like this. Not when Mrs Leavengate died so recently ... I think it's horrible of you.'

'Why horrible of me? I'm not going to hook Philip.' Dereck's voice turned reflective. 'If she believes the local rumour she must be quite grateful to Elizabeth – if local rumours reach as far as the south of France.'

Kate bit her lip. 'I don't believe that rumour. It's the kind of malicious gossip you always get when a person has that kind of an accident.'

Dereck shrugged. 'On a night that wasn't fit for a dog to be out Elizabeth goes for a walk along the cliffs and the wind blows her over the edge to her death. Come off it, it'd be a miracle if there weren't rumours of suicide.'

She knew he was right but loyalty made her argue on. 'But why should she have committed suicide? She and Philip were happily married – everyone knows that.'

'I'm not saying they weren't. But she was acting strangely the last few months. She'd be too lethargic to get out of bed for days on end and then suddenly she'd get a furious fit of energy when no one, not even the doctors, could stop her going for long walks along the cliffs. The doctors thought it was due to her disease she had some mysterious kidney trouble they couldn't cure – but I'm not certain it was as simple as that.'

In spite of herself she was intensely curious. 'What do you mean?'

There was a frown around Dereck's slightly petulant mouth. 'There were all kinds of things... For one, you must have heard how friendly she had become with Mrs Treherne – they were often seen whispering together as if they had some secret... And she always took these curious impulsive walks in the evenings when Philip was working late here in St Marks – I can't think why but it's a fact that she did. I know the coroner gave her the benefit of the doubt but I don't think even Philip is absolutely sure. Are you?'

She ignored the question. 'Where do you pick up all this gossip?'

'Things get around, darling. You have other staff at Whitesands and you employ charwomen – they all see things and chatter. And so one hears these things.'

'It's strange I've never heard any of them,'

she said coldly.

His voice was malicious, punishing her for her contempt. 'Not so strange, darling. People wouldn't talk to you – they recognise you as the loyal type.'

His mockery was beginning to anger her. 'None of these things in themselves prove she committed suicide any more than Caroline's coming to Whitesands means she is trying to hook Philip, as you put it. Couldn't she just be paying a visit to show her sympathy?'

His smile was cynical. 'I've only met Caroline twice but I'd say there was as much sympathy in her as blood in a stone. Plenty of synthetic sympathy, mind you I'll lay odds she's a good actress.'

'If you've only met her twice, how can you be so sure? You're getting to be nothing but a scandal-monger, Dereck. Thirteen years is a long time – she must have made lots of men friends since then.'

'I don't doubt that she has, darling. But she still isn't married, is she? And let's face it' – Dereck's voice was faintly insinuating – 'there aren't many women around who wouldn't throw a hook after Whitesands and Philip.'

Seeing she was distressed now as well as angry his voice lost its malice. 'I'm joking – you know darned well I don't think you're that type. Let's stop talking about Elizabeth, Caroline, and everything to do with Whitesands. I'm much more interested in getting you to come out with me one evening next week. What about it? I'll behave myself – I promise.'

She managed a smile, wondering how much her own doubts about Caroline had helped her in forgiving him so quickly. 'We'll see. I'll give you a ring if I feel like going out.'

She was relieved when Dereck had to return to his office: it was difficult to make light conversation with her mind full of the things he had told her. She no longer felt like shopping but among other things she badly needed a new costume. It proved more difficult than she had expected to find one that suited her, and by the time she had bought a small present each for John and Sarah it was nearly one o'clock.

She found herself driving slowly back to Whitesands as if afraid Caroline had already arrived and she wanted to postpone meeting her as long as possible. But the house looked as solid and impassive as ever from the main road and when she approached it along the cliffs and saw nothing unusual her confidence began to return. She turned the car into the drive and drove it round the side of the house. As she rounded the corner of the east wing her heart gave a sudden thud and began beating rapidly. In front of the twin garages was a sleek foreign sports car. And leaning against it, talking animatedly to Philip and an excited Sarah, was a woman Kate knew could only be Caroline.

She was tall with long, nylon-clad legs and graceful gesticulating hands. A slim-fitting fawn costume showed off the shapely perfection of her figure. Round her throat she wore an emerald chiffon scarf, a foil for her built-up blonde hair. She looked as exclusive and sleek as the sports car against which she was so elegantly leaning.

The sound of Kate's arrival made her turn her head. Kate, motionless in her seat for the moment, caught a glimpse of a beautiful face with high-arched brows and a full red mouth. Then Philip's voice made her start.

'Come over and meet Miss Worth, Kate. She got in five minutes ago.'

Kate swung the door back, jumped out, and made her way towards them.

2

Philip introduced them. 'Carol, this is Miss Fielding, whom I've been telling you about. Kate, this is my wife's cousin, Miss Worth.'

Kate had not failed to notice the sudden watchfulness of Caroline's green eyes at the appearance of another young woman. As she paused alongside Philip and caught the fragrance of expensive perfume, she wondered whether she ought to offer her hand and a second later was glad of her hesitation when Caroline remained leaning elegantly against the sleek sports car.

'Oh, hello.' Caroline's voice, animated a moment ago when talking to Philip, was suddenly languid. 'You're the children's nurse, Mr Leavengate tells me.'

Kate tried her best to sound relaxed. 'Yes, that's right. I'm very glad to meet you, Miss Worth. I've heard so much about you, particularly from Sarah here.'

She was grateful for Sarah's presence, taking the attention of the other two away from her for a moment. Sarah's oval face was flushed with excitement as she clutched a child's pearl necklace. 'Look what Aunt Caroline's brought me, Kate. Isn't it lovely?'

Kate bent down to examine the expensive present. 'It is beautiful, dear. Aren't you a lucky girl?'

'She brought John an aeroplane and a kite,' Sarah went on breathlessly. 'The kite's super. He's run off to show it to Mr Wirral.'

Philip's voice was amused. 'You look as if you're going to get some exercise this afternoon, Kate.'

Kate was turning to him when Caroline's voice came between them like a silken screen. 'You seem lucky with your employees, Phil. I understand you're very satisfied with Mrs Treherne too?'

Kate was grateful to Philip for his look of embarrassment. 'Yes; she's been excellent. She's a splendid cook.' He glanced at the house. 'Would you like to go inside now? Wirral will have got your things upstairs and it won't take Mrs Treherne long to prepare lunch for you.'

She nodded, detaching herself elegantly from the car. 'Good idea – I'll go and freshen up.' Bending down she chucked Sarah under the chin with a beautifully manicured hand. 'Don't go far away, my chick. We've lots of things to talk about.'

She gave Kate a nod as she turned away. Philip's voice – Kate wanted to believe it was more friendly than ever to compensate for Caroline's detachment – reached back to her. 'Don't bother to put the car away, Kate.

I'll be wanting it later this afternoon.'

The gravel was not suited to Caroline's stiletto heels. After a few steps she gave a low laugh and put a hand on Philip's arm to steady herself. They looked a handsome couple as they made for the house, the tall, dark figure of Philip and the exquisitely slim, blonde woman. Sarah hesitated, threw a half-apologetic glance up at Kate, and then scampered after them.

Kate returned to the car. As she reached it John came running out of the house towards her, his small shoes scrambling excitedly across the gravel. He was carrying a large kite in his hand which he held up breathlessly to Kate.

'Look, Katie. Look what Aunt Caroline has given me.'

It was a type of kite Kate had not seen before, patently expensive with revolving blades like a helicopter and plastic tail fins. She took it from him and pretended to examine it with interest.

'It's splendid, darling. Aren't you a lucky boy?'

He nodded vigorously. 'I got an aeroplane too. But it's all in pieces and has to be put together. I'm going to ask daddy to do it for me.'

She handed him back the kite. 'That's right, dear. But give him a little time. Auntie Caroline has only just arrived and he has to see she gets lunch first, hasn't he?'

John nodded and turned his serious blue eyes up to her. 'Did you go into the shops, Katie?'

She felt her muscles tighten. 'Yes, dear. I've just come back.'

The blue eyes held her own with the terrifying frankness of the very young. 'You said you were going to get me a surprise, Katie. Are you going to give it to me now?'

She tried to speak but failed. Dismay spread over his guileless blue eyes like a film of oil. 'You didn't forget, did you, Katie? You couldn't have, 'cause you promised…'

She reached blindly into the car and pulled out two parcels. John's face lit up again as she handed him one, and he dropped the kite. As his stubby eager fingers tore off the paper wrapping she closed her eyes. His muted cry of disappointment seemed to come from far away. 'Why, it's not a surprise, Katie! It's only another kite. A little one…'

She could not remember afterwards what words of comfort she gave him. For at that moment the two kites, the cheap one and the expensive, seemed cruelly symbolical as she locked the car and made her way to the house.

Kate saw little of either Philip or Caroline that afternoon but in the early evening, as she was putting John to bed, Philip came up into the nursery.

'Hello, Kate. I've come to say good night to John. I have to take a run into town before dinner and he'll probably be asleep when I get back.'

John was sitting up in bed, his face rosy from his evening bath. On a chest of drawers alongside him were the toys he had received that day, among them his new aeroplane. Philip went over to him and ruffled his fair hair. 'Good night, son. Sorry I can't read you a story tonight. Be a good boy and sleep well.'

'Have you thanked daddy for putting your new aeroplane together?' Kate asked him.

As John was thanking him Philip turned to Kate. 'I hear you bought each of them a present this morning, too.'

She coloured and busied herself by tucking in the blankets at the foot of John's bed. 'They were nothing. Just two very small things.'

He stared at her. 'What do you mean – small? Presents aren't judged on their size. You shouldn't spend so much of your money on the children, but it is very kind of you.' For a moment he seemed about to say more. Then he called a last good night to John and left the room.

There weren't many men, she thought, who would have noticed... But she had already learned he was that kind of man. Her eyes were still slightly misted when she watched his car drive round the front of the house. She had half expected Caroline to be with him but he was alone.

His words, with their implications, were still warming her when she began reading a bedtime story to John. She had just finished the first page when Sarah came running down the corridor.

'Kate. Aunt Caroline wants to speak to you.'

Without understanding why Kate felt her heart start beating faster.

'Where is she, dear?'

'She's in the library.'

Kate hesitated, tempted for the moment to make Caroline wait until she had finished John's story. Then she turned to Sarah. 'Be a good girl and read the rest of this story to John, will you? I'll be back as quickly as I can.'

She ran downstairs, tapped on the library door, and entered. Caroline was seated in one of the hide armchairs by the fireplace. She had dressed for dinner and was wearing a halter-necked, low-cut evening gown. Two emerald combs, set in either side of her built-up blonde hair, matched her green eyes. In the late sunlight that slanted through the French windows she was a picture of perfect grooming, and yet to Kate she seemed oddly out of place in the oak-panelled, leather-upholstered library. At the same time she could believe a man would see only the perfection of the woman's figure and the frozen beauty of her face.

Kate paused by the door. 'You wanted to see me, Miss Worth?'

Caroline turned. 'Oh, yes. Please come in, will you?'

To Kate's surprise, as she approached the fireplace, Caroline held out a gold cigarette case to her. When she refused Caroline took a cigarette herself. Through a haze of smoke her green eyes surveyed Kate.

'Mr Leavengate has taken a quick run into St Marks and before he returns for dinner I thought I'd like a word with you. He tells me you do some secretarial work here as well as look after the children. What exactly does that mean?'

Kate explained how she paid the wages of the staff and looked after their insurance cards and income tax deductions. Caroline's plucked eyebrows arched.

'Is that all? Mr Leavengate made it sound as if you did quite a good deal of work.'

'There are quite a number of other things,' Kate admitted. 'If Mr Leavengate wants anything for the house or the farm I order it for him. Or I may have to advertise for temporary farm labour for Mr Marsden, the farm manager. It's difficult to list all the things I do – they vary so much from week to week.'

Caroline nodded. She flicked ash into the

fireplace and then turned to Kate. 'I may be staying at Whitesands some time, Miss Fielding, and I'm not the sort of person who likes idling her time away. So on Monday I'd like you to run over all these things with me so that in the future I can handle them myself. It'll give me something to occupy my mind and leave you more time for the children.'

It followed so well the pattern Kate had expected that she had a numbed feeling of fatality. 'But there's no need for that, Miss Worth. The children aren't any trouble – I can manage the rest easily enough.'

Caroline's green eyes lifted. Behind the haze of cigarette smoke Kate could not be certain whether or not there were faint mocking lights dancing in them.

'Mr Leavengate tells me you have been working too hard since you've been here. So I'm quite certain he'll approve of the arrangement.'

The last thing Kate wanted to do was make an enemy of her. 'It's very kind of you to offer, of course. But you do understand my position – I shall have to get his approval first.'

Caroline's cigarette left a lazy line of smoke as she waved a confident hand. 'You can leave me to make everything right with Mr Leavengate.' Her tone changed. 'What are you doing now – putting John to bed?'

'Yes, I was reading him a story.'

Caroline tossed her cigarette into the empty fireplace and rose. 'You can take a break, if you like. I brought a few books with me for the children – I'll take one in and read to him myself.'

Kate hesitated. John was a sensitive, affectionate child and for months had not gone to sleep without a story from her. Yet she did not see how she could object without appearing churlish.

'Yes, of course. Sarah's reading to him at the moment. I'll go up and tell him you're coming.'

Caroline, evening dress rustling, went to the door. 'Don't bother. I'll get the book now and go straight in. And don't forget – on Monday morning we'll run over the secretarial work together.'

Kate nodded silently and followed her from the room.

Dinner, which was delayed an hour because of Philip's excursion into St Marks, was an ordeal Kate would gladly have missed. Although in Philip's presence Caroline was studiously polite to her, she nevertheless managed to convey her disapproval at having to share the table with an employee in a way that no woman could mistake. Without Sarah's chatter to use as a distraction – the child had already eaten and been put to bed

– Kate suffered considerable embarrassment which the plainness of her simple grey costume against Caroline's glamorous gown did nothing to dispel, and for the first time in months she was glad when the meal was over and she could retire to her room.

Before getting into bed she took her last look at the children. John had been unusually restless that evening – after Caroline had finished reading to him a story he had insisted on seeing Kate again – and now, as she stood over him, he muttered something in his sleep and flung himself over in the small bed. Tucking the blankets around him again Kate waited to assure herself he was sleeping soundly again before retiring to her room.

It was just after one in the morning when she heard a sharp, frightened cry. Switching on her light she ran barefoot into the nursery. John was sitting upright in bed, his eyes wide and terrified although she could see he was still asleep. As she reached the bed he dropped back, muttering in a feverish voice. Bending down she put an arm around him. 'What is it, darling? What frightened you?'

'Mummy,' he moaned. 'Mummy, come on. Get up...'

She felt her heart contract. 'Darling, what's the matter? Wake up and tell me.'

Her voice awakened him. Immense relief flooded into his terrified eyes as he stared

40

up at her.

'Everything's all right now, darling,' she whispered. 'It was only a dream, that was all.'

Fear still drifted like silt in his defenceless eyes as he stared up at her. 'Oh, Kate, it was awful… An ugly man with a sword was chasing mummy and me through the trees. And mummy fell down and I couldn't get her to move…' His voice changed. 'Where is mummy, Kate? Why don't we see her any more?'

Kate found difficulty in speaking as she held him close. 'Mummy has had to go away to God, darling. But she looks after you and loves you just the same. It was only a silly dream you had – there's no ugly man chasing you.'

His hot cheek pressed against her arm. 'I'm ever so glad you're here, Kate. Ever so glad…'

She stayed with him until he was asleep again. As she rose from his bedside she noticed a new book lying among his toys on the chest of drawers. Realising it must be the book Caroline had been reading from she took it back into her room. It was of American origin – she guessed Caroline had bought it on the Continent – and the stories it contained, all of violence in the Middle Ages, were utterly unsuitable for a boy of John's age. Remembering Caroline saying she had brought other books with her Kate realised she would have to be warned of their harmful effects on a mind as impressionable as John's. It was a thought disturbing enough to keep Kate herself awake and restless half the night.

The following morning, Sunday, Kate took Sarah to the small church in Pennon Cove. On their return to Whitesands there was still an hour to pass before lunch and as the weather was perfect the children persuaded her to play a game of cricket with them on the back lawn. Kate was just running in an effort to catch the ball that Sarah had hit high into the air when Philip came through the shrubbery that lay between the lawn and the garages. Surprised at his sudden appearance she stumbled and only his outflung arms prevented her falling.

'Steady,' he laughed. 'If you play games as hard as this you'll break your neck.'

The hint of admiration in his voice deepened the colour of her flushed cheeks. 'I'm sorry. I didn't notice you coming.'

'Of course you didn't.' It was his turn to show embarrassment now. 'Kate, I hope you don't mind missing Synon Cove today. I promised to take Carol for a run this afternoon to see some of the local beauty spots.'

He was referring to a cove eight miles along the coast which had an excellent beach for bathing. The children loved the cove because it had a number of large and exciting caves which they never seemed to tire of exploring, and for the last two months Philip had made a habit of taking them and Kate on Sunday afternoons for a swim there. She had liked to believe he enjoyed these afternoons as much as herself – certainly it had become her highlight of the week.

Now, however, she felt no surprise. Since Caroline's arrival she had known that unless Caroline was to accompany them the outings could no longer take place. At the same time she could not help feeling disappointment.

'Of course not,' she heard herself saying. 'Why should I mind?'

Sarah had run up to them and heard their conversation. 'Can't Kate come with us too, daddy? There's plenty of room in the car, isn't there?'

Kate intended refusing quickly before he could speak, but his reply was immediate. 'Of course she must come, darling. I was only explaining why we couldn't go to Synon Cove today, that was all.'

Had he known Caroline would not want her with them and had Sarah forced him into making the offer? Kate did not know although his voice and smile seemed sincere enough. But in any case the thought of an afternoon sharing the car with Caroline was unthinkable.

'It's very kind of you, but I think I'll stay home this afternoon. I've lots of odd jobs to do for myself – things I've been putting off for weeks.'

As she spoke she thought she caught a movement in one of the rear windows of the house, but when she turned her gaze on it she could see nothing.

Philip had turned to pick up the ball from the shrubbery where it had rolled, giving her no opportunity to tell whether he was relieved or sorry at her refusal. 'Are you quite sure?' he asked as he turned and tossed the ball to Sarah. 'We shall be back earlier than usual – round about five. And you don't get out very often, you know.'

'Really,' she smiled. 'It's very kind of you but I would rather stay at home today.'

As he nodded slowly she realised it was an ideal opportunity to ask him whether he wanted her to hand over the secretarial work of the estate to Caroline. But at that moment Caroline appeared at a rear door behind the house and called him. He acknowledged her, then turned to Kate. 'You'll have to excuse me now but I promised to take a look at some of Carol's colour slides of Italy. Sorry again about this afternoon – I shall miss our swim myself.'

Kate was at least certain of one thing as she watched his tall figure stride towards the house. Caroline had noticed the two of them in the garden and had come out deliberately to break up their conversation.

Left alone that afternoon Kate spent the first hour taking up the hem of her new costume which under careful scrutiny had proved too long. By three o'clock it was finished and as the weather had stayed fine she decided to take a walk along the cliffs. On reaching the hall she saw Mrs Treherne walking across it with a pile of newly-ironed linen over her arm, and on an impulse Kate approached her.

'Hello, Mrs Treherne. You ought to be out this afternoon – it's such beautiful weather.'

The stocky, dark-visaged housekeeper turned, her expression showing no response to Kate's friendliness. 'People eat on Sundays like any other day, miss.'

Kate nodded sympathetically. 'That's true. Then can I help you with anything? I'm quite free this afternoon and was only going for a walk.'

The woman shook her head doggedly. 'No, thank you, miss. You've got your job and I've got mine. I don't need any help.'

It was a direct rebuff but Kate tried to turn it. 'I suppose you've heard that Mr Leavengate will be home earlier than usual today?'

'Aye. Miss Worth told me. About five, she said.'

In spite of herself Kate had wondered if Caroline's interference had been directed at her primarily because she was the only other

45

young woman at Whitesands or whether it was only a part of a general move to gain control of the household. Her question came out before she could check it.

'Have you spoken much to Miss Worth yet, Miss Treherne?'

The housekeeper's small black eyes turned on her quickly. 'Spoken to her? What do you mean, miss?'

The sharpness of the question took Kate aback. 'I mean, has she made any alternative suggestion to you about the running of the house?'

'No, of course she hasn't. Why should she?'

The housekeeper's bluntness made Kate feel a gossip, and her cheeks were burning as she turned away. 'It doesn't matter – it's not important. If there's nothing I can do to help you I'll go for my walk now.'

She felt the housekeeper's suspicious eyes following her as she left the kitchen. Outside the air was fresh on her hot cheeks: there was a slight breeze off the sea. She took the cliff path towards Pennon Cove which led her up the opposite headland of Whitesands Bay and gave her a magnificent view of the rugged coast and blue sea. The cliffs to the east, ahead of her, appeared deserted with only a derelict summer house breaking the wildness of the view. It had been built for Philip's grandmother, who had been something of a recluse, but since her death it had fallen into disuse. It stood perhaps fifty yards back from the cliff edge, enclosed by a wooden fence that had been breached in half a dozen places by the wind and weather. As Kate came opposite it she saw a man lying in a hollow at the cliff edge. He gave her a wave and she recognised the spare figure of Wirral. His crooked face showed pleasure as she sank into the grass alongside him.

'What are you doing?' she smiled. 'Having a lazy afternoon in the sun?'

He nodded, jerking a cigarette-stained thumb in the direction of Whitesands. 'So you didn't get to Synon Cove today?'

'No, not today. Mr Leavengate has taken them for a ride instead.'

'You mean she's taken them for a ride, don't you?' he grunted.

Although she felt Wirral could be trusted, her recent experience with Mrs Treherne had left her cautious. 'I suppose it's quite natural Miss Worth should want to see the beauty spots. After all, she only arrived yesterday.'

His husky voice was sardonic. 'She's been here before, you know, miss. Plenty o' times.' His bushy eyebrows lifted challengingly. 'What do you think of her, Miss Kate? Fair and square.'

Kate hesitated. 'I don't know... As I said, she only came yesterday – it's much too early to judge yet.'

'She's wasted no time pushin' her weight around,' Wirral muttered. 'Only two hours after she'd come she told me the windows were dirty. And I'd only done 'em on Wednesday ... I never liked her. Too haughty-taughty and full o' foreign ways for me.'

Relieved she appeared not to be the only object of Caroline's interference, Kate laughed. 'You're just prejudiced because it was through her that Mrs Treherne came to Whitesands.'

'And isn't that reason enough?' Wirral grunted. 'Do you trust a woman kids don't like? I don't.'

'The children, Sarah anyway, seem to like Miss Worth well enough. So on your argument you ought to like her, even if you don't like Mrs Treherne.'

'I don't like either of 'em,' Wirral muttered. 'And don't worry, Sarah'll find her out soon enough. Kids don't take long to see through people.'

Although Kate liked Wirral she knew he was a born grumbler and so could not be taken too seriously. 'Why do you dislike Mrs Treherne so much? She's really an excellent cook and housekeeper, you know.'

This praise for his enemy appeared to resolve a long-standing hesitation in Wirral's mind. He glanced around him, then leaned forward. 'Miss Kate, I'm goin' to tell you something I haven't told a soul before –

there's something queer about that Treherne woman. You wasn't here when she came, so you won't know, but it wasn't until after that Mrs Leavengate started takin' those queer walks along the cliffs in the evenings. I often used to see the two of 'em whisperin' together and once I saw both of 'em come to that place yonder,' and he jerked his head at the summer house behind them.

Kate stared at him, remembering what Dereck Redfearn had said about the strange intimacy that had appeared between Elizabeth and Mrs Treherne and wondered if Wirral, in spite of his denial, had been the source of the disclosure. 'But what was so strange about the two of them going to the summer house?' she asked. 'It belongs to the estate – perhaps Mrs Leavengate wanted it cleaning out or redecorating.'

Wirral shook his head with conviction. 'No; it was nothin' like that. They didn't see me – I was lyin' here in the grass – and that woman Mrs Treherne was whisperin' somethin' to the mistress and pointing to the path that comes up from the road. It looked queer, it did – the mistress was lookin' very upset – and it wasn't more 'n a few weeks after that when the poor soul flung herself off this very cliff. Something queer was goin' on, miss, I'm sure of it.'

So he believed Elizabeth had committed suicide too... The knowledge, added to the reminder that the tragedy had taken place on this very headland, brought a sudden chill to Kate. 'You said she "flung herself" from the cliffs. Are you saying she committed suicide?'

Wirral was immediately on the defensive. 'I never went as far as that, miss. I meant fell off the cliffs – it was a slip o' the tongue.'

She knew he was not telling the truth. 'Have you ever mentioned anything of this to Mr Leavengate?'

'No, miss; I haven't told anyone. There didn't seem anythin' concrete enough and I wouldn't want him to think I was blackenin' the woman's name for nothing.'

Kate nodded slowly. 'It probably was nothing important. It couldn't have been or Mrs Leavengate would surely have told her husband.'

It was clear Wirral did not agree but by tacit agreement both of them dropped the subject, he out of alarm he had said too much, Kate for less definable reasons. But fifteen minutes later, when she left the gardener to continue her walk, the things she had heard followed her like shadows, and it was a relief to reach Pennon Cove where the jostling crowds of holiday makers served to distract her mind. It was well after four-thirty when she left the cove and knowing the children might already be home she took the bus back. It dropped her off on the main road and to reach Whitesands she took a short cut across the estate. She had just climbed a stile over the last stone hedge and was about to emerge from a thick bank of rhododendrons that screened the end of the garden when she heard the sound of muted voices.

Something about their tone made her pause. Peering through the screen of leaves she gave a start of surprise. Standing together in the garden behind a large bush as if intentionally screening themselves from the house were Mrs Treherne and Caroline. Their appearance suggested they had been quarrelling. Mrs Treherne looked sullen and unco-operative and, most surprisingly of all, Caroline looked less haughty than irritable. After another minute of muted arguing they appeared to reach a reluctant agreement. Mrs Treherne nodding dourly and starting back for the house, Caroline remaining behind the bush. She looked her age now, lines of displeasure marring the beauty of her face as she drew irritably on a cigarette.

At last she threw the cigarette away and turned for the house, taking a different path to Mrs Treherne. To Kate, watching her go, the mystery of Whitesands deepened. What strange part had Mrs Treherne played in the life of Elizabeth Leavengate before her tragic death? And what connection did she have now, a housekeeper at Whitesands, with the glamorous and haughty Caroline?

3

The first hint of the conflict that was to develop between Kate and Caroline occurred that evening when Kate was putting John to bed. As always when Philip was home he came upstairs to say good night to the child and tonight Caroline accompanied him. She had already dressed for dinner and her bronze satin frock rustled expensively as she passed Kate on her way to John's bedside.

After she and Philip had chatted a few minutes to the solemn-faced child she turned to Kate. 'You needn't bother to stay, Miss Fielding, if you have any other work to do. I'll read him his bedtime story.'

Kate gave a start, regretting now she had not yet mentioned the unsuitability of the book Caroline had given John. Sensing the resentment Caroline might feel if mention were made before Philip she did her best to avoid trouble by taking another book from the chest of drawers and handing it to Caroline.

'This is the book we've been reading this week, Miss Worth. We've reached chapter four.'

Caroline glanced at it, then at Kate. 'I gave him a new book last night. May I have it, please?'

Kate felt herself go hot and cold. 'I took that one away, Miss Worth. It's in my room.'

Caroline gave an amused laugh. 'Don't tell me that you read children's adventure stories?'

You're cruel, Kate thought suddenly. Cruel for the sake of being cruel, like a lovely sleek cat. Controlling her resentment she said quietly: 'No; that wasn't my reason, Miss Worth.'

'Then what was your reason? Fetch it for me, will you, please.'

Kate's embarrassment was made no easier by the knowledge that Philip was also staring at her curiously. She hesitated, then motioned to the door. 'If you wouldn't mind stepping outside for a moment, Miss Worth, I'll explain.'

Caroline turned and lifted her bare shoulders at Philip. 'My dear; the mystery the girl's making over a child's book. I'm becoming quite fascinated.'

She swept past Kate into the corridor. Kate followed her, inwardly praying Philip would stay with John. But he, thinking her reticence to talk in the nursery was due to John's presence there, followed her outside.

There was a hardness about Caroline's curiosity as Philip closed the nursery door, sealing all three of them in the corridor. 'Well – now you've got us outside, what is all this mystery about the book?'

Kate realised there was no hope now of keeping the matter from Philip and took a deep breath. 'I'm sorry, Miss Worth, but I don't think that book is suitable for John. After you read him a story from it last night he was very restless and during the night he had a nightmare about men with swords chasing him through a forest.' For Philip's sake she omitted to mention the child had also dreamed of his dead mother. 'I realise you couldn't know this before, but John's a very sensitive child and easily excited before bedtime. That was why I took the book away.'

The look she feared had come into Caroline's eyes – small green flames of dislike. 'Are you telling me you understand John better than I, Miss Fielding? This isn't my first visit to Whitesands, you know I've read him bedtime stories before.'

'I know that, Miss Worth, but I'm certain it was the book that upset him last night. He was almost feverish when I went in to him.'

Caroline's red lips twisted in amused contempt. 'All boys like adventure stories. You've been reading too many articles on child psychology in the Sunday newspapers, my dear.'

Kate's protest was out before she could

check it. 'I've not been reading any articles in the Sunday newspapers, Miss Worth. I've had John in my care for five months now and I know what upsets him.'

'And I don't know – is that what you're saying?' Behind her amused facial mask Caroline's eyes were ice-hard. 'You're a very outspoken girl, aren't you?'

Philip's interruption came as an immense relief to Kate. 'Now just a moment – both of you.' Although he spoke with a laugh there was an undertone of firmness and authority in his voice that brought the situation back under control. 'As I see it, there's nothing to get heated about. You both want the best for the child, so it's simply a matter of finding out who's right. Fetch the book, will you, Kate, and let me look at it.'

Kate brought it from her room and handed it to him. Caroline had regained control of herself now and was busy lighting a cigarette. Through the haze of smoke she realised Kate could feel her assessing eyes, staring as though seeing her for the first time.

After a seemingly endless half-minute Philip looked up and smiled ruefully at Caroline. 'You know, Carol, Kate's quite right. This book's much too violent for a little chap of four and a half. He's barely out of the Bunny Rabbit stage yet.'

To Kate, watching almost fearfully, Caroline's expression seemed to blur like a film going in and out of focus. Then she turned a face showing only regret and concern to Philip.

'I've made a mistake, have I? I saw the books in Paris on my way here and I thought they'd be just the thing for a boy.'

'They probably would be, for an older boy. But apart from his age John's very sensitive, as Kate says, and anything exciting before his bedtime makes him restless.'

Her lovely face was all contrition now. 'It was silly of me, I see that now. But I don't see John very often and when one hasn't any children of one's own it makes it rather difficult to judge these things.'

He would not have been the man he was if her words, delivered with the faintest undertone of sadness, had not brought a warm response. 'Forget it, Carol. No great harm's been done. Has it, Kate?'

His question brought Kate back into the circle from which she had been temporarily felt excluded. 'No, of course not. I realised Miss Worth didn't know. That was why I wanted to speak to her alone...'

Seeing her distress Philip turned and put a reassuring hand on her arm. 'Stop worrying about it. Carol knows you were only looking after the boy's interests.'

Although he had taken her side in the argument Kate's insecurity had made her fear he might secretly resent being forced into such a stand, and it was a comfort to hear his reassurance. At the same time it brought a new fear. Did he not realise what he was doing, standing close to her with his hand on her arm, while Caroline waited unattended behind him?

She could not help moving her head nervously to see past Philip's broad shoulders. Again her impression was momentary – as fast as a camera shutter – but again it seemed Caroline was staring at her with animosity through the haze of smoke. The moment was over faster than the telling; Philip dropping his hand from her arm and stepping back, Caroline, all shapely shoulders and scented femininity, moving towards the nursery door. Her shapely lips smiled ruefully at Philip.

'I'm going in now to read John that Bunny Rabbit story. So if he has nightmares tonight it must be my face that frightens him and not the stories I read.'

Philip's laugh expressed his appreciation of her recovery. 'If that gives him bad dreams, Carol, then he'll never turn out into the man I'm hoping he'll be.'

At the door Caroline turned back to Kate. 'I think I owe you an apology, Miss Fielding. You were only doing your duty and I was rather impatient with you. You'll have to blame it either on the weather or my quick temper.'

It was a handsome apology for what had happened, and Kate would have given much to believe it sincere. But at that moment she felt her worst fears had been realised, that Caroline would not forgive her for the incident, and the fact she was prepared to apologise in front of Philip seemed to make her animosity only the more dangerous.

When Kate went downstairs it was past seven-thirty and she could see nothing of Sarah. On Kate's arrival back from Pennon Cove Sarah had asked permission to go and play with her friends Mary and Betty Dundas, and as there had still been two hours to dinner Kate had agreed. Mary and Betty were the young daughters of a doctor who had recently bought a villa on the eastern boundary of Whitesands and they and Sarah had become good friends. To reach one another the girls cycled along a footpath that ran eastwards along the boundary of the fields.

Seeing nothing of Sarah in the garden Kate walked up the front drive and turned down the footpath. Two hundred yards from the house the path dipped, giving a view over the estate and a chance to see if Sarah were making her way home yet.

The mossy grass outside the gates of Whitesands fell away as the footpath led Kate between the high hedges that bounded the fields. It was a perfect summer evening, sun-lit, mellow, and so quiet she could hear the church bell at Pennon Cove, ringing for the evening service. Tiny scufflings sounded in the bushes alongside her as birds began settling down for the night and in the evening sunlight the ripening brambles hung in shiny red clusters. Through a gap in the hedge she caught sight of Wirral's bachelor cottage, a neat stone building in the fields near White-sands with its garden gay with flowers.

At that moment Sarah came round a bend in the path, pedalling her bicycle hard. She was panting, her shoes and frock were dusty, and there was a smear of dirt across one flushed cheek. Her expression showed she had been enjoying herself.

'What have you been doing?' Kate asked as the girl braked and jumped down. 'We shall be late for dinner if we're not careful.'

'Sorry, Kate,' Sarah panted. 'But I was having such fun with Billy I forgot the time.'

Kate stared at her. 'Haven't you been playing with Mary and Betty, then?'

Sarah shook her head. 'No. As I was going to their house I met a boy playing near the old summer house. Oh, he's ever such fun, Kate... He can do cartwheels and walk for miles on his hands. And you should see the boat he's got. Cut it all out from a block of wood...'

When Sarah was excited her chatter took a

good deal of controlling and Kate held up a hand in protest. 'Wait, darling. Who is Billy? How old is he?'

'He's eleven, the same as me. He lives in Bristol or somewhere.'

'But what was he doing near the summer house. Didn't he know he was trespassing?'

Sarah's excited eyes clouded. 'No. He says he's often cycled out here before when he's come to St Marks and no one's ever told him the cliffs were private.'

'You mean he comes to stay with relatives in St Marks?'

Sarah nodded. 'He says he was last here at Christmas. This time he's here 'cause he's been sick and has to have a week's holiday. He goes back next Sunday.' Her eyes pleaded with Kate. 'Daddy won't mind him playing here, will he? He might come again next weekend before he goes back.'

'Of course he won't – not if Billy is a nice boy. But I do think your father would like one of us to meet him. So next time he comes, bring him to the house for a lemonade, will you, darling?'

'All right; I will. If he's able to come again... Oh, I do hope he can, Kate. He's ever so nice.'

'I'm sure he'll be back again soon,' Kate comforted her. 'Now do hurry or we're going to get into trouble with Mrs Treherne.'

Sarah's chatter ceased as if a tap had been

61

turned off. Mentioning Mrs Treherne, Kate thought, was like invoking the legendary bogey man, and as they walked back to the house, Sarah pushing her bicycle, she could not help the question: 'Why do you dislike Mrs Treherne so much, darling? She's never been really unpleasant with you, has she?'

It was a few seconds before Sarah answered. She kicked a stone sullenly off the footpath. 'I suppose not, really... She's just horrible, that's all. I wish she'd never come to Whitesands.'

'Do you mean it's her manner that upsets you? You shouldn't take that too seriously, you know. Some people are naturally dour like that.'

Sarah shook her head moodily. 'No, it's not only that. I just don't like her, that's all.' The glance she threw at Kate was suddenly apprehensive. 'Why do you want to know, Kate?'

Since her mother's death there was an insecurity about Sarah that showed at odd moments. Sensing it now Kate laughed. 'I've no real reason, you silly girl. I was just wondering, that was all.'

Back at the house they found Mrs Treherne waiting to serve dinner. After apologising to her Kate sent Sarah to wash. While the girl was absent she took the opportunity of mentioning Billy to the housekeeper.

'He sounds a nice enough boy but I've

told Sarah to bring him here the next time so we can meet him. I thought I'd mention it to you in case I should be out at the time.'

Mrs Treherne's dour face showed her disapproval of all trespassers, children or otherwise. 'She oughtn't to play with any child she comes across, Miss Fielding – especially ones that don't get permission. Goodness knows what she might pick up from them.'

Kate ignored the interference in the housekeeper's advice, feeling it was probably provoked by their lateness to dinner. She had little idea as she led Sarah into the dining-room of the all-important part the innocent Billy was to play in the future drama of Whitesands.

The weather broke the following morning. Rain was falling steadily from a grey sky when Kate waited with Sarah inside the side porch while Philip backed the car from the garages. Sarah was wearing her full school uniform: a navy-blue skirt trimmed with a narrow band of green, a navy-blue mackintosh and a panama hat. Over one shoulder she was carrying a satchel.

Condensation fumes rose from the car's exhaust as Philip turned it on the gravel apron behind the house and pulled up in the drive. He jumped out and ran towards her, rain-drops glistening on his uncovered black hair. Kate drew Sarah aside to allow him to enter the porch. He grinned at her wryly.

'It's a proper Blue Monday, isn't it?' He turned to Sarah. 'Well, young lady. Are you ready to go?'

Sarah, who disliked school, nodded gloomily. 'Yes; I suppose so.'

Philip winked at Kate. 'Cheer up – another few weeks and you'll be on your summer holidays. Talking about holidays, Kate, reminds me… Yesterday afternoon, when we were out in the car, Carol mentioned she'd suggested taking some of the secretarial work from you. Apparently she hasn't any plans yet to resume her travels and feels she'd like to make herself useful about the place. How do you feel about it? As she says, it'll take a bit of the weight off your back.'

Again Kate had the feeling of fatality, of being an actor in an over-rehearsed play. 'I don't know why you all think I've been over-worked – I've never thought so. But if you feel you'd like her to take the work over I'll show her all I can.'

His gaze was suddenly very penetrating, making her look quickly away. 'Now wait a moment,' he said quietly. 'Make certain you understand the reason I'm doing this. It's not because of any dissatisfaction – you know perfectly well you've done a wonderful job. But you know I've been wanting to lighten the load for months now and this is the ideal opportunity.'

Because he genuinely believed her load was too heavy she could bear him no resentment for holding his ground. He couldn't see the ultimate outcome – she knew that.

'Yes, of course I understand,' she said dully. 'I'll run over everything I do with Miss Worth this morning.'

Sarah broke the slight tension. 'Does that mean Kate'll have more time to play with us, daddy?'

Philip, as relieved as Kate at the interruption, tweaked the girl's ear humorously. 'Definitely, darling. And more time to take a day off when she feels like it.' He glanced at his watch. 'It's time to be going. Where's that little scamp John run off to?'

'I'll fetch him,' Kate said hurriedly. A moment later she returned with John, who was clutching a piece of toast in one small hand. 'Say goodbye to your daddy. He's going off to work now.'

As John held up a solemn cheek for Philip to kiss, Kate caught sight of Caroline, wrapped in the glamorous morning coat she had worn at breakfast, watching them from the hall. Her expression, almost feline in its intentness, became one of sophisticated mockery on noticing she was observed, and she sauntered gracefully down the corridor towards Philip.

'If everyone else in the house is making

such a fuss of your going, I'd better do the same,' she murmured, eyes flickering on Kate. Her slim hand went out to Philip. 'Have a good day, make lots of money, and don't be late home.'

After John had waved goodbye to the departing car and Kate was turning for the hall, Caroline checked her. 'Mr Leavengate approves my taking over the secretarial work, by the way. Has he mentioned it to you yet?'

Half of Kate's mind could not help taking in her appearance at close quarters. To achieve that casual, just-out-of-bed look she must have risen at least half an hour before the rest of them… 'Yes,' she said quietly. 'He told me this morning. What time would you like me to run over it with you?'

Caroline shrugged. 'Shall we say about ten-thirty? In the library.'

It was just eleven o'clock that morning when Kate closed the top drawer of the big library desk. 'I think that covers all the routine things, Miss Worth. Of course, as I told you on Saturday, I do get other work as well. But Mr Leavengate always explains everything very fully.'

Caroline was sitting on the arm of one of the hide armchairs, a cigarette in one hand. She was wearing an emerald cashmere sweater and slim-fitting slacks, and with her blonde hair piled high with combs she looked more decorative than competent. But even if she had not guessed it earlier Kate knew from the alert way she had picked up information that a shrewd brain lay behind the mobile, lovely mask of her face.

Caroline nodded, blowing smoke out through her nostrils. 'Have you got any of these miscellaneous jobs running at the moment?'

Kate reached down to the second drawer of the desk. 'Yes; I still have to show you this graph,' and she pulled out a folder containing a pile of foolscap papers. A large folded graph lay among them and this Kate opened out and laid on the top of the desk.

Caroline left the armchair and stared down at it. 'What on earth's all that about?'

'It's an experiment Mr Leavengate is doing for the local Agricultural Board,' Kate explained. 'Recently a new hormone food for dairy cattle has been developed – it's supposed to increase their milk yield and Mr Leavengate has agreed for six of his animals to be given the food and their yield compared with his other cattle.' Kate pointed to the lines on the graph. 'As you see it didn't seem to make any appreciable difference for the first few weeks but recently there has been a definite improvement.'

Caroline was still gazing down at the graph. 'I suppose everyone's quite excited about this?'

'I think they are,' Kate admitted. 'Particularly Mr Leavengate. I understand he went to school with the man who asked him to carry out the experiment, and if it turns out a success it will improve his friend's chance of promotion.'

Caroline lifted her cigarette to her amused red lips. 'Sounds typical of Philip – always feeding other people's stray cats. Who gives the dairy returns to you? Marsden?'

'Yes. I get them every day and put them in this drawer.'

'I suppose you enter them on the graph every day – if one or two were missing it would upset the whole experiment, wouldn't it?'

'Oh, yes; it would. But I can't enter them every day – it's a fairly complicated business because it has to be worked out with the lactation period of each animal and Mr Marsden helps me on that. We usually do it every Friday evening.'

Caroline's lips twisted in distaste. 'Cows and milk – it sounds pretty boring to me. How much longer has the experiment to run?'

'Quite a few weeks yet, I'm afraid.'

'Then I think if you don't mind you'd better continue with it until it's finished. I don't want to muscle in and spoil things.'

Her willingness to put Philip's interest

before her own came as a surprise to Kate and made her wonder for the first time if her judgment of her had been over-harsh.

The rest of the week followed without incident although, with less work to do, Kate found time dragged more slowly. Except in the evenings she saw comparatively little of Caroline. Since coming to Whitesands it had been Kate's custom to take lunch alone with John when Sarah was at school, and as Caroline spent most of the weekdays out in her sports car, their only regular contact was over dinner in the evenings when Philip was present, a situation very much to Kate's liking.

On Thursday she remembered her promise to Dereck Redfearn and phoned him at his office. 'I don't believe it,' he said. 'You've remembered... What night are you having dinner with me?'

Kate hesitated. 'What nights will Mr Leavengate be working late this week? Do you know?'

'His usual nights, I suppose – tonight and tomorrow.' Dereck's voice became malicious. 'Why? Can't you tear yourself away from him when he's home?'

She felt like putting the receiver down. 'It's just the opposite – I can only go out when he's here.'

'Why?'

'It's because of Sarah – I don't like leaving her alone. I'll explain another time.'

'And so, as Philip usually goes out on Saturday nights too, you've got yourself an excuse for not coming out with me this week. Is that what you're telling me?'

'I'm sorry, Dereck – it's not my fault.'

'All right, all right. Then what about next week. Early – when the lord and master is in. Say Monday?'

'If he's home, yes. May I confirm it and let you know?'

'Do that, darling. And if you can't make it, arrange for either Tuesday or Wednesday. You see what a faithful swain I am.'

The weekend came and brought good weather. On Saturday morning Sarah had barely finished breakfast before she asked Kate if she might go off and play. Kate guessing the reason, smiled.

'All right – off you go. But remember – if you see Billy bring him to the house for a glass of lemonade.'

Sarah, pretty in a pair of jeans and a yellow pullover, was off like a sprinter from a starter's gun. 'Thanks, Kate. I won't forget.'

Shortly afterwards, as Kate was cleaning up the nursery, John came in to see her. 'Katie. What're you doing?'

She turned at the sound of his solemn voice with its attractive lisp. 'I'm tidying up your room, darling. Why?'

70

Sadly he held up a jam jar filled with water. A tiny dead fish floated mournfully upside down on its surface. 'My fish is dead, Katie. Will you take me to the beach so I can get another?'

Kate glanced at her watch. It was nearly ten-thirty and she felt that if Sarah didn't bring Billy to the house soon it meant the boy had not managed to get to Whitesands that morning.

'All right, darling. In half an hour's time we'll go down.'

John's solemn face peered at her watch. 'Is half an hour very long, Kate?'

'No, darling. When this hand reaches the top, see. Not long. Now you go and play in the garden until I call you.'

When Kate went outside at eleven o'clock Philip was driving his car out of the garage. As he passed her and John on the front drive he stopped and leaned from the window. She noticed his gaze run appreciatingly down her figure, trim in a beach shirt, shorts and sandals.

'Hello; where are you two going? Down to the beach?'

Kate pointed to the empty jam jar. 'We're after tiddlers. Percy has passed away.'

His blue-grey eyes twinkled at her. 'Oh, that's bad news. Never mind, maybe you'll catch a crab or two this morning. Wirral says the pool under the big rock is full of them.'

'We'll do well if we catch another Percy,' Kate told him. 'I'm no fisherman.'

He reached out and rubbed John's head affectionately. 'I wish I could come down with you both this morning. But I've a client to see. Is there anything you'd like bringing back from town?'

'I don't think so, thanks.'

Her eyes followed his car as he drove through the gates. His friendliness had cheered her and for the moment she forgot her anxieties as she turned to John. 'Come on, darling. I'll race you to the end of the drive.'

It was a steep climb down to Whitesands Bay, the fish in the rock pools proved elusive, and it was almost twelve-thirty when they regained the house. A bicycle, propped up against a laurel bush in the side drive, told Kate Sarah was home. Philip was not back yet and Kate noticed the red sports car was also missing from the garage – Caroline must have gone out after they left.

As they entered the hall, John carefully carrying the precious jar containing Percy the Second, Kate saw Mrs Treherne descending the staircase. The housekeeper's small black eyes darted on them, but she gave no sign of recognition as she turned away. Kate watched her curiously. Her face, always dour, was unusually set and there was a strange air of agitation about her as she hurried towards the kitchen.

Leaving John to take his fish into the play-room Kate went upstairs to change. As she started down the corridor she heard the sound of muffled sobs coming from Sarah's room. Startled she ran into it, to find Sarah outstretched on her bed, crying as if her heart would break.

Kate tried to turn to girl's face towards her. 'What's the matter, darling? What's happened?'

It was a full minute before she could get a coherent word from her. 'I did as you said, Kate. And it's spoiled everything... Oh, I hate her...'

'You hate whom? Mrs Treherne?'

Sarah nodded, lifted her tear-stained resentful face. 'Yes. I brought Billy here and she was horrible to him. She told him to go away and that if he ever came on the estate again she'd call the police.'

'The police! But why?'

'I don't know except that she told me I ought to be ashamed of playing with anyone like that... It's not true, Kate. He's nice. She only did it 'cause she hates me...'

Kate spent another minute comforting her and then rose from the bed. 'Stay here, darling. I'll go and speak to her. I won't be long.'

Kate went into her room and pulled a frock over her beachwear. Then she went downstairs. Although resolute her face was slightly pale. There was an uncompromising quality about Mrs Treherne that made even a slight complaint an ordeal to deliver. As she pushed back from the kitchen door the housekeeper was reaching into a cupboard. She appeared occupied and yet something about the set of her strong body told Kate she was braced for trouble.

Kate steadied herself. 'Mrs Treherne. I want to speak to you about Sarah.'

For a long moment the housekeeper did not move. Then she turned slowly. Her swarthy face was both threatening and defiant as she faced Kate. 'Well, miss. What is it?'

'I think you know. The child's upstairs crying her eyes out. What was your reason for being so sharp with this friend of hers?'

The effect of her words surprised her. The woman's small eyes flickered as though with sudden fear. 'Reason? What do you mean, reason?'

'Why did you send him away and threaten him with the police if he came on the estate again? He wasn't trespassing – I told Sarah to bring him here.'

Relief flooded into the small black eyes, bringing back truculence with it. As the housekeeper strode towards her and Kate braced herself for the quarrel that appeared imminent, the mystery that lay over Whitesands seemed to deepen. Why was this dour,

74

normally impassive woman afraid of an unknown eleven-year-old boy who did not even live in the district?

4

Mrs Treherne looked a formidable figure in her austere black dress as she approached Kate. Her blunt, almost masculine voice was aggressive now. 'I didn't send him away only because he was trespassing. I sent him off because he wasn't the right sort to play with Sarah.'

'What do you mean – he wasn't the right sort?'

'What I said. I know a bad 'un when I see one. He was rough an' he was rude.'

'In what way was he rude?'

The housekeeper's scowl deepened. 'Have you see him yourself?'

'No. That was why I asked Sarah to bring him to the house.'

'Well, I *have* seen him. And I'm telling you now he's not the right sort to play with her.'

Kate was determined not to be browbeaten by this truculent uncompromising woman. 'Just the same you had no right to send him away like that. You should have let him stay until one of us got back.'

Mrs Treherne's arms folded. 'Last Saturday you told me to look out for him if Sarah brought him round. It wasn't my fault you were down enjoyin' yourself on the beach this morning.'

Kate's face went pale with anger. 'Where I go is a matter between myself and Mr Leavengate – no one else. Just as the care of the children is my business too. And I'm not going to have either of them frightened by you, Mrs Treherne. Sarah's in a terrible state this morning – I've never seen her so upset.'

'Of course she's upset. She hasn't had her own way. But you can't give in to children just because they throw a fit of tears. You ought to know that, miss.'

Kate went to the door, turned back. 'I'm perfectly aware children can't always get their own way. But I also know there are ways and ways of handling affairs like this. I'm not saying the boy was suitable to play with her, but I do think you ought to have given one of us the opportunity of seeing him too. And you certainly shouldn't have threatened him with the police. Mr Leavengate is the last person to have children frightened like that.'

Her mention of Philip halted the housekeeper's aggression. 'You don't know that kind of boy like I do, miss,' she muttered sullenly. 'They don't take any notice of you unless you threaten 'em.'

'I don't know anything about the boy but I do know that the care of the children is my responsibility. So in the future I'd be grateful if you'll leave me to handle matters of this kind in my own way.'

Kate could feel the housekeeper's hard black eyes boring into her back as she turned and went down the corridor into the hall. Upstairs she found Sarah had partly recovered and was sitting up on her bed, although her swollen eyes remained as evidence of her distress. They filled with a lugubrious curiosity as Kate entered the bedroom.

'What did she say, Kate? Was she horrible?'

Kate sat on the bed and took the girl's cold hand. 'I want to talk to you about Billy, darling. What kind of a boy is he?'

The girl's forehead puckered. 'I've already told you. He's nice – ever so nice.'

'Yes, but is he a rough sort of boy? Does he speak badly and use strange words?'

'No, of course he doesn't. He's got a bit of an accent but that's nothing, is it? You've always told me no one should judge a person on the way they speak.'

'That's quite right, dear. But he must have been rude in some way to Mrs Treherne. What exactly did he do?'

Sarah's face showed instant dislike and understanding. 'So that's what she said. Well, she's lying. He didn't get a chance to be rude to her – I wish he had... As soon as she saw him she went for him. She said he was a trespasser and that if she ever saw him

around the estate again she'd call the police.'
Sarah's blue eyes filled with tears again.
'Why did she have to say that? He never
refused to go…'

As Kate comforted her again she heard
the sound of an approaching car. Turning to
the window she saw Caroline's red sports
car nearing the gates of the drive. Caroline,
cool and chic at the wheel in a yellow shirt
with a green chiffon scarf at her throat,
might have been the model for a glossy car
advertisement. Remembering the strange
intimacy she had noticed between her and
Mrs Treherne the previous weekend Kate
had a sudden impulse and went to the door.
'I have to go downstairs for a moment,
darling. Why don't you go into the playroom
with John? He's very proud of the fish we
caught this morning.'

She ran downstairs into the empty hall. She
hesitated between the two closed doors of the
sitting-room and the library, finally choosing
the latter and leaving the door slightly ajar
behind her. She ran over to the French
windows but Caroline's car had already
vanished round the side of the house. As she
stood there she heard hasty footsteps enter
the hall. Crossing quietly over to the door she
listened. The footsteps were hurrying over to
the side corridor that led to the porch and
she knew they belonged to Mrs Treherne. A
moment later a distant door opened and

closed. Half a minute passed and the door opened again and she heard the whisper of voices. They were pitched too low for her to make out what they were saying but an urgency about them was unmistakable. Twin pairs of footsteps – one with the tap-tap of high heels – crossed the hall in her direction to die away on the carpet that ran down the corridor to the kitchen.

Kate stepped out into the hall and approached the corridor. It was empty: Mrs Treherne and Caroline had gone into the kitchen. Hating herself for what she was doing and yet impelled by a curiosity stronger than herself Kate tiptoed a few yards along the corridor. She heard the women's voices again. The closed kitchen door kept their meaning from her but could not hide the anxious, almost feverish urgency behind them. Kate wanted to go as far as the door itself but realised, almost with a shock, that she was too frightened. As she stood there, heart hammering, she heard Caroline's voice rise on an angry, dominant note. For a moment the women appeared to be quarrelling, then their voices fell away until they could scarcely be heard.

Hastily Kate backed away down the corridor and re-entered the library. A moment later she heard the sharp tap-tap of heels on the tiled floor of the hall. They half-crossed it, hesitated, there was the snap of a cigarette lighter, and then the footsteps headed straight for the library door.

Kate flew across the room to the desk, pulled out her pile of returns and pretended to be scanning through them. Through a wall mirror above her head she could see the door. It swung back and Caroline appeared.

Inhaling deeply on a cigarette as she stood in the doorway she did not notice Kate immediately. She was barely recognisable as the chic, composed woman Kate had seen driving the sports car a few minutes earlier. The nerves of her face had tightened, drawing the skin over the bones so that it formed hard protuberances and taut lines. Her forehead was furrowed and her mouth hard as she tugged repeatedly at her cigarette. Her green eyes stared into the smoke she exhaled as though searching for an answer to a sudden and dangerous problem.

Then she noticed Kate and her slim body tensed and swung round like a cat scenting peril. 'What the devil are you doing in here?' Her voice was a whiplash, quite different from her usual sophisticated drawl.

Heart thudding, Kate turned towards her. 'I'm going through my returns, Miss Worth. Why? Is anything wrong?'

Caroline's face was catlike as she assessed the degree of danger. For a few seconds the silence in the library was unbearable. Then her lovely mask fell back into place as she regained control. Only her eyes remained watchful as she moved gracefully towards an ashtray on a chair arm.

'There's quite a lot wrong, from what I hear,' she drawled. 'I understand you and Mrs Treherne have been having words over a boy Sarah brought round here this morning. She was full of it when she met me at the door just now...'

You're clever, Kate thought. Clever and needle-sharp. You know I must have heard you and Mrs Treherne in the hall and so you're telling me as much of the truth as you can... But why – what is the connection between you and Mrs Treherne and an unknown eleven-year-old boy?

She nodded, struggling hard to control her nervousness. 'Yes, I had to speak to her. When I came up from the beach Sarah was terribly upset – apparently she had brought the boy here as I asked and Mrs Treherne had shooed him straight off the estate. I think she went too far – particularly when she threatened him with the police – and I told her so.'

'Have you seen this boy yourself?' There was a sharpness about Caroline's question that made Kate feel it was somehow disassociated from the conversation.

'No; and I feel I ought to have been given the chance. Mrs Treherne knew I wouldn't be away for long.'

Caroline's tight nerves seemed to slacken at her answer, erasing some of the tiny lines left around her mouth. 'Of course if the boy was as rough as she says, it's perfectly true Sarah can't be allowed to play with him.'

Her poise, with lowered eyes staring down at the ashtray at which she tapped her cigarette with a manicured finger, was a thoughtful one but Kate was certain her thoughts were not what they seemed.

'I realise that,' she said quietly. 'But I do feel one of us ought to have had a chance to see for ourselves. As things are this has only made Sarah dislike Mrs Treherne more than ever.'

Caroline looked up sharply. 'What do you mean – more than ever?'

'I thought you knew. Sarah has always disliked her. In fact dislike is hardly the word – she's afraid of her.'

The green eyes were dagger-sharp again. 'Why? She's always behaved well, hasn't she?'

'Oh, yes. She's an excellent housekeeper.'

'Then why doesn't Sarah like her?'

Kate hesitated. 'I don't know. Possibly because she's so dour and unfriendly... I don't think Sarah really knows herself.'

Almost imperceptibly Caroline's slim body was relaxing again. 'In other words it's nothing but a child's prejudice?'

'I suppose it is, in a way,' Kate admitted. 'But it's very real to Sarah and this affair over the boy will make things worse. That's one reason I wish she hadn't taken so much into her own hands.'

A brief silence followed in which Kate could hear the piping of a blackbird outside. Then Caroline's voice came again. 'This boy' – one of her tapered hands was toying with an ashtray on the chair arm – 'Mrs Treherne said something about his living in Bristol. Is that true?'

'That's what Sarah says.'

'Then how does he come to be down here?'

'Apparently he has relations in St Marks and sometimes comes to stay with them during his holidays.'

'But surely the schools there haven't broken up yet, have they?'

'Sarah says he has been ill and has been having a week's convalescence. He goes back home tomorrow.'

'But he may come back again during his summer holidays?'

He's very important to you, this unknown boy, Kate thought. But why? Why?

She nodded. 'Yes; I suppose he might.'

The slim hand playing with the ashtray seemed to tighten for a moment. Then Caroline straightened, shrugged and moved gracefully towards the door. 'Well; if he is so rough and badly-behaved, we shall have to keep Sarah away from him if he's disobedient enough to come round here again. You'll tell her this, of course.'

Kate could not contain all her rebellion. 'If he's as bad as Mrs Treherne makes out, naturally I should keep her away from him. But if he comes here again I'd like to make sure by seeing him myself. Or by letting Mr Leavengate see him.'

Caroline, turning towards the door, seemed to freeze. Her expression was hidden from Kate but the air seemed suddenly charged with static. Kate found herself holding her breath in the few interminable seconds before Caroline turned back to her, her voice cold with reproach.

'I think you'd be well advised to keep this affair in proportion, Miss Fielding. Mr Leavengate is particularly busy at the moment – he is handling a very important case – and I don't want him bothered by staff quarrels, especially one over an unknown boy. Whatever other faults Mrs Treherne may have, I can't see why she should lie about him, and if she says he is not fit to play with Sarah, that ought to be good enough for you. She is not to see him again and there the matter is closed. Is that quite clear?'

It was well conceived, Kate thought, pretending the affair was little more than a petty staff quarrel and so below Philip's attention. But there are things the best actress cannot hide, and long after Caroline had left her

Kate felt chilled and oddly afraid.

Sarah, dejected and at odds with the world, did not stray far from the house for the rest of the day and as far as Kate could tell Caroline made no attempt to talk to her about Billy. The following morning after church Sarah asked if she might fill in the two hours before lunch by going to play with Mary and Betty. It was a usual request and Kate saw no reason to refuse it. Sometime after Sarah had gone, however, although Philip was home, Kate noticed no sign of Caroline in the house. She kept her eyes open and just after twelve o'clock noticed Caroline and Sarah returning together along the path that led across the estate to the doctor's villa. Sarah, pushing her bicycle, seemed oddly subdued and went straight up to her bedroom on reaching the house. After a few minutes Kate went upstairs to see her.

The girl was sitting on the bed with lack-lustrous eyes, an open book lying beside her. She gave a start on hearing Kate and turned towards the book, pretending she was reading it. Making certain the door was closed Kate went over to her.

'Darling,' she said quietly. 'I want to talk to you for a minute. Did you see Billy again this morning?'

The start the girl gave told Kate her guess was right. She sat on the bed. The sullen way the girl faced her told Kate she expected to be reprimanded, a thing odd in itself. Kate took her unwilling hand.

'I'm not angry with you, darling. I guessed Billy might have arranged yesterday to say goodbye to you – that was one reason I let you go off this morning.'

Sarah's reaction puzzled her. Biting her lip the girl turned away. 'I wish I'd never gone. I don't want to see him again – ever.'

'Why, dear? Was he nasty to you?'

Sarah's chestnut hair shook. Tears were glistening in her eyes.

'Then why do you wish you'd never seen him?'

Sarah did not answer. Kate waited a moment and then tried another approach. 'Where did you meet him? On the estate?'

Sarah shook her head again.

'Then where, dear?'

'On the road that runs to Dr Dundas's house,' the girl muttered.

Kate tried to keep her voice casual. 'And where did you meet Aunt Caroline?'

Sarah swung round in surprise. Kate saw her tearful eyes were strangely evasive. When she did not answer Kate tried again. 'We don't have secrets from one another, do we, darling? Tell me what happened this morning. Did Aunt Carol see Billy? Or did you meet her afterwards?'

'Afterwards,' Sarah muttered.

'So she doesn't know any more about him than I do?'

The girl's hesitancy told Kate she was holding something back. 'She didn't see him, if that's what you mean.'

'And yet you never want to see Billy again. I'm afraid I don't understand, darling. Was it something he said or did this morning? Or was it something that Aunt Carol said about him afterwards?'

Sarah suddenly flung herself on the pillow, sobbing. Distressed, Kate tried to take her hand. The girl pulled it away. 'I don't want to talk about him any more. Leave me alone – please.'

'But what's the matter? What did Aunt Carol tell you about him?'

'It's nothing … I just don't want to talk about it, that's all. Please leave me alone, Kate…'

Kate could do no more than comfort her until her tears ceased. The net of mystery that lay over Whitesands now appeared to have ensnared Sarah and Kate's apprehension grew as she went out into the garden to call John for lunch.

It was not until after dinner that same day that Kate remembered she had not yet spoken to Philip about her Monday night engagement with Dereck Redfearn. She felt diffident about telling him and it was not until late that evening, on meeting him leaving his study, that she made the plunge.

'Mr Leavengate, will it be all right if I go out tomorrow evening? I'll put John to bed before I go.'

Philip looked as if he had been working hard. His movements were weary and his black hair slightly dishevelled, reminding Kate what Caroline had said about the important case he was working on. 'Of course it'll be all right, Kate. And you don't need to worry about John – one of us can see to him. Would you like to borrow the car? I don't expect I'll need it, but if I do I can borrow Carol's.'

'No, thanks – I'm being picked up.' Ever since making the engagement she had known she must tell him, yet now the words seemed to stick in her throat and she was glad the hall lights had not yet been turned on. 'It's Dereck Redfearn – he's calling for me.'

He seemed to stiffen. 'Dereck?'

The dusk hid his expression but she felt certain it was one of displeasure. Her efforts to explain only made her embarrassment worse. 'We're only having dinner ... I shan't be late home.'

He turned away. 'It's not my business what you do, Kate. And you don't have to hurry back – this isn't a remand home.'

His brusqueness worried her, making her wonder if he had some objection to members of his household staff becoming friendly with his business partners. It made her next question more difficult to ask. 'You say you won't be wanting the car – does that mean you're definitely not going out?'

Seeing his stare and feeling her question bordered on impertinence her voice ran on quickly. 'I mean, if you are I would stay in. Another night would do just as well for me...'

'I don't expect to be going out, no. But would it matter if I did? The children wouldn't be alone – Mrs Treherne would be in. And probably Carol, too.'

She threw a quick nervous glance around her. The hall appeared deserted although the shadows were thick where the corridor ran to the kitchen. 'I'd rather not go out if you aren't certain you'll be here. It's not in the least bit important to me...'

He had not missed her anxious stare around the hall. Giving a puzzled frown he nodded at the sitting-room door. 'You'd better come along and tell me what the trouble is, Kate.'

It was the last thing she wanted, particularly as she believed Caroline was in the room. Yellow light washed over her as Philip opened the door for her to enter. She saw the drawn brocade curtains, the soft wall lights, the lush suite with its deep empty armchairs, and it took her apprehensive mind a moment to realise that Caroline was absent.

Her feet sank into the deep carpet as Philip led her to one of the armchairs. 'What about a glass of sherry?' he asked. 'You're looking rather pale.'

She nodded nervously. 'I'd love one, thank you.'

She watched his tall figure move over to a cocktail cabinet that stood near the window. Her mind was struggling to decide how much she should tell him: the situation had developed so quickly she had no idea what was the wisest course to take and it seemed mere seconds before he was back and handing her a glass of sherry.

'Drink that off. It'll do you good. And what about a cigarette?'

She seldom smoked but now she felt she would do anything to stall for time. 'Thank you. I would like one.'

He cocked a half-amused, half-curious eyebrow as he handed her his case. The smoke bit her throat as he leaned down and gave her a light. The wall lamps, with their shadows, brought out the tiredness of his strong face, the latent humour of his mouth. 'Don't try to inhale – that's only for confirmed smokers. Just draw it into your mouth and blow it out again.'

She felt her cheeks grow hot and took a hasty sip of sherry. He went to the armchair opposite, sat forward with his elbows on his knees, both hands clasped around his glass. 'Well, now you're comfortable, tell me what's worrying you about Sarah.'

She took a deep breath. 'It's nothing, really. I just don't like leaving her without one of us being here.'

His eyes were keen, analysing her expression. 'You must have a reason. Is it Mrs Treherne?'

She felt as if she were sitting in a car without brakes and rolling ever faster downhill. She nodded without speaking.

'You mean it's because of this dislike Sarah has for her?' As she nodded again he frowned. 'But surely it hasn't got so bad we can't leave them alone in the house together. Mrs Treherne has never been unkind to her, has she?'

He did not miss her slight hesitation. 'No – at least not deliberately, I don't think.'

'And yet you think Sarah is afraid to be left alone with her. Why? There must be a reason.'

Kate was thinking of Caroline. If she once mentioned the boy Billy to Philip, Caroline would believe it deliberate and then, instinct warned her, the war would really begin... 'She's afraid of Mrs Treherne – she always has been. It's much worse than you think... I don't think there was ever a concrete reason – it was just there. But it's very real to her and I can't bear the thought of her lying upstairs and frightened.'

She had not convinced him that was all: she saw at once although under its firmness his voice was appreciative of her concern for Sarah. 'And of course that mustn't happen. But there's been something to bring this to a head – I could tell that in the hall. What is it, Kate? I want to know.'

Everything that had happened since Caroline's arrival had made Kate feel she was being swept helplessly along in a swift-flowing current. There was no possibility of denial now – he had only to question Sarah to discover the truth and because of Sarah's strange behaviour she did not want that. Some inner self-protective mechanism sealed off thoughts of the consequences as she began to explain.

'Last weekend Sarah told me she had met a boy of her own age playing near the old summer house – apparently he's down in Cornwall convalescing from some illness. I thought we ought to see what kind of a boy he is and so I told her to bring him to the house the next time he came. She brought him yesterday morning when I was on the beach and Mrs Treherne saw him instead. Apparently she didn't like him and told him to get off the estate and that if he ever came back she'd call the police. Sarah liked him very much and was most upset.'

Philip was frowning heavily. 'She threatened an eleven-year-old boy with the police. Why?'

'I spoke to her about it and she said it was because he was very rough and rude. I don't doubt she meant well, but I felt she'd taken too much on herself and we had a few words about it. That doesn't matter, but I am worried about the effect on Sarah. She disliked Mrs Treherne enough before...'

Her voice stopped short. She had believed the sitting-room door closed – now she noticed it was a few inches ajar. And she thought she had heard the faintest noise from the hall outside...

Philip was watching her closely. 'What's the matter?'

It cost her a great deal to continue without faltering. 'Nothing. I was just saying that it has made things worse and that's the reason I don't like leaving Sarah alone with her.'

Philip's eyebrows were knitted together. 'You've never seen this boy yourself?'

She shook her head.

'So, apart from what she's told you, we've no other witness the boy is so badly-behaved...' For a moment his voice was thoughtful. 'And she can be a cantankerous old devil, I know that...'

He nodded abruptly, finished his sherry and rose. There was a decisiveness about his movements that alarmed Kate. 'What are you going to do?'

'I'm going to have a talk with her. We'll see what she has to say for herself. She'll have to learn a little tact – I'm not going to have Sarah upset for nothing. Nor, for that matter, am I going to have children scared off the estate by threats of police action. That's too much. You ought to have told me straight away, Kate.'

Both reason and instinct told her he was right and yet now she found herself blindly defending the woman. 'She probably meant well. But she has such a dour and awkward manner...'

He ignored her. 'Where will she be now? In her quarters?'

'I don't know. I suppose so.'

He went to the bell-push alongside the fireplace, then shook his head and turned to the door. 'I'll go and see her. You wait here.'

His words were like a signal. Footsteps sounded in the hall outside, the door swung open and Caroline appeared. She looked as if she had just returned from a walk, wearing slacks and an expensive-looking suede jacket over a green shirt. She spoke in an amused sophisticated drawl. 'Hello. Is this a tête-à-tête or may I join you?'

Philip ignored her banter. 'Sit down and have a sherry with Kate. I'll only be a few minutes.'

Kate, her mouth dry, noticed she was still standing between him and the doorway. Her

96

high-arched eyebrows lifted solicitously. 'You're looking a wee bit peaky, darling. Is anything wrong?'

'Mrs Treherne has been throwing her weight around a little and I'm going to talk to her, that's all. Kate'll tell you all about it.'

He turned to stub out his cigarette in a nearby ashtray and as his attention was diverted, Caroline threw a glance at Kate. It was a split-second glance but it came like a flung dagger, vicious with menace, and Kate knew her worst fears were realised. Then Philip turned back and the lovely face was all concern again. 'It isn't about a little boy called Billy, by any chance, is it? You're not angry because she sent him away?'

5

Philip stared at Caroline. 'Do you know something about this boy, too, then?'

Caroline moved forward now, away from the doorway. 'Yes; I heard quite a lot about the affair when I got home yesterday morning. Mrs Treherne met me at the door.'

'It seems everyone in the house knows about it but me. Did she tell you why she'd sent the boy away and threatened him with the police if he came back?'

'Oh, yes – everything. She was quite upset.' Caroline's eyes, bland now, flickered on to Kate. 'Apparently there'd been a little trouble about it.'

Philip nodded curtly. 'Kate feels she took too much on herself and I agree. That's why I'm going to see her.'

'Of course,' – Caroline's voice was almost apologetic in its insinuation. 'Miss Fielding hasn't met this boy or even seen him, has she?'

Philip threw a glance at Kate who was still sitting as though made of stone. 'I know that. But one hasn't to see a child to know he oughtn't to be sent off the estate like a criminal. Or Sarah to be upset.' He started for the door. 'I won't be long. Pour yourself a sherry and give Kate another one, will you.'

Caroline sighed and followed him. 'I think I'd better come with you, darling. There are a few things you ought to know.'

He paused, frowning. 'What other things?'

She took his arm. 'I'll tell you as we go. Come along.'

Kate, seeing the door close behind them, could still see the glance Caroline had thrown at her on entering the room. It had been as malevolent as the stare of a cat whose prey had been frightened away. But why? Why had it been so important to her that Philip should not hear about the boy?

Almost dully Kate wondered what story she was now fabricating for Philip. For although her acting had been brilliant Kate had seen the urgency behind it. Philip's interest in the affair had to be utterly destroyed and to that end Caroline would apply all the resources of her needle-sharp mind.

Lost in thought she did not know how many minutes passed before the door opened again and Philip and Caroline entered. It took all her courage to lift her eyes to Philip's face and his expression confirmed all her fears, being cleared of everything but a faint disappointed perplexity as he glanced at her.

'I've had a word with Mrs Treherne, Kate, and from all I hear it is perhaps best the boy is kept off the estate in the future.'

Kate's voice was unsteady as she rose from her armchair. 'You think now she was quite right in sending him away like that?'

There was a certain brusqueness about his reply. 'I don't say she was right in the way she handled it I've told her that. But what I didn't know was that Carol saw the boy herself this morning, talking to Sarah near Dr Dundas's house. And from all she tells me I'm satisfied he's not the type of lad we want playing with her.'

She lied to you, Kate thought. She never saw the boy at all – Sarah told me that... Seeing the gleam of mockery in Caroline's eyes Kate suddenly wanted to hear no more.

Halfway to the door she turned back to Philip. 'You do realise that this won't affect Sarah's opinion of Mrs Treherne? That she'll still be just as afraid of her?'

He gave a brusque nod. 'I know that. But I can't very well punish the woman when I'm satisfied she had Sarah's interests at heart.'

'I never asked you to punish her,' she reminded him quietly, wondering what other poison Caroline had spread. 'My only concern is Sarah. I don't want her frightened.'

His face cleared again. 'I know that, Kate, and don't worry. I'll make certain one of us is here on Monday and any other evening you go out. Feel better now?'

She tried to return his smile. 'Thank you.

Good night.'

To reach the door she had to pass Caroline. She avoided her eyes but the woman's perfume followed her out into the hall like some sweet and deadly poison.

By the evening of the following day Kate wished she had never agreed to have dinner with Dereck. Sarah had not yet recovered from her strange, evasive behaviour and Kate would have given much to have stayed with her in an attempt to regain her confidence. Instead she had to dress and by the time she had put John to bed Dereck was due.

As she stood at the nursery window, watching the front gate, she was glad she had asked Dereck to wait outside for her. After Philip's brusqueness the previous evening on being told she was going out with Dereck she felt it would be almost an act of hostility to let him drive right up to the house for her. And yet why, she wondered? Why should she feel guilty merely waiting for the car to arrive...?

She had the same feeling of guilt five minutes later when she hurried down the staircase, hoping to gain the side porch unseen. The very rustle of her dress sounded almost furtive and she winced at the at frivolous tap-tap of her evening shoes on the tiled floor of the hall. She saw nobody as she ran down the corridor to the side door, only for her relief to turn into dismay as she

102

stepped out on the drive. Both Caroline and Philip were standing there alongside Caroline's red sports car, which had the bonnet raised. Kate was as certain Caroline had arranged the encounter as she was certain of the woman's insincerity as she turned and tilted her blonde head appreciatingly sideways.

'How pretty, dear. Your boy friend's very lucky – don't you think so, Phil? Doesn't she look nice?'

Kate's face burned painfully as she hurried up the drive, noticing Philip did not round the house to greet Dereck. Already she felt her evening had been spoiled but for Dereck's sake she made an effort to be sociable. They dined well in one of the best hotels in St Marks and afterwards Dereck took her out on the glass-enclosed veranda. By this time dusk was falling in the narrow, old-world street outside, cosy with its ancient stone buildings and warm street lamps. As they sat over a liqueur Kate found her thoughts straying back to Sarah.

What was it Caroline had told the girl yesterday that had made her so evasive? Before she had always confided in Kate, and it hurt to discover that confidence appeared to have gone. And because it was connected with the mysterious Billy it alarmed her too…

Dereck's voice made her start. 'You've

been staring out of that window for nearly five minutes. A penny for 'em, darling.'

She reached hastily for her glass. 'I'm sorry, Dereck. I'm afraid I'm not very good company tonight.'

Dereck, his lanky figure immaculate in a charcoal grey suit and silk tie, grinned at her wickedly. 'What is it – the Cannes bombshell? How is she getting on, anyway? You haven't said much about her tonight.'

Kate stared down at her glass. 'What do you want me to say? That she's everything you said she was?'

He grinned again. 'That's one of those remarks that can be taken two ways. What's the matter, darling – is she beginning to push your nose out?'

She badly needed someone to confide in and had his reply been less malicious she might have told him everything. As it was she bit her lip and turned again to the window, just in time to notice a long grey car nose out from a nearby street and head down the road. Noticing her start, Dereck turned his head.

'That's Philip's car, isn't it?' he asked.

Her anxious eyes were following the receding car. 'I think so. But I understood he was staying in tonight.'

Dereck shrugged. 'Perhaps he'd been called out by a client. You get the odd cranks, you know, wanting their will changed in the middle of the night after a family quarrel. We've one old boy, Sellick, who changes his every three months. It could be him – he's about due.'

'Then you don't think Caroline was with him?' At his sardonic expression her voice became impatient. 'No; it isn't that, you idiot. It's Sarah. I don't want her to be left alone.'

'I couldn't see if she was with him or not. But why are you worried about Sarah? You've got the housekeeper on duty, haven't you?'

On reflection she felt certain Philip would not leave Sarah alone with Mrs Treherne – not after what he had told her. But knowing the strange intimacy that lay between Caroline and Mrs Treherne, were things any better with Caroline there? Could Caroline be trusted not to go for a walk, for example... Impulsively she reached out and put a hand on Dereck's arm.

'Don't be angry, Dereck, but would you mind taking me home? I'm sorry, but it's very important to me.'

'Go home – now! But it's isn't ten o'clock yet.'

'I know and I'm terribly sorry. I'll explain on the way back.'

For a moment his good-looking face was sullen with disappointment. Then, seeing her expression, he gave a shrug and rose. 'All right – I suppose there's no point in keeping you here against your wishes. Come on, then.'

As the lights of St Marks fell behind their car she tried to explain. 'I don't know if you've heard, but Sarah's frightened of Mrs Treherne. It's the reason I never go out in the evenings when Philip isn't home – I can't bear to leave the poor child alone in the house with her.'

'But surely she'll be in bed and fast asleep by this time.'

'She'll be in bed – she promised me to go up at eight-thirty. But if she heard her father go out before she fell asleep and she believes herself alone with Mrs Treherne she'll lie up there frightened stiff.'

'But doesn't Philip know about this?'

'Oh, yes! I've mentioned it more than once. But I'm not sure he realises how bad it is – I didn't myself until recently. He promised me either he or Caroline would stay in tonight, but I can't trust Caroline – she thinks it's just a silly childish obsession and might easily go out for a walk.'

At the gates of Whitesands she turned to him. 'Thanks for a wonderful dinner. And I'm terribly sorry about this. You do understand?'

He held her back. 'I'll understand on one condition. That you'll come out with me again next week.'

She felt unable to refuse. 'All right. Ring me on Monday.'

'And I want a good night kiss. You can't refuse me that, either.'

'No, I can't.' Before he realised what she was doing she leaned quickly forward and kissed his cheek. Then she jumped from the car and ran down the shadowy drive.

The east side of the house was in darkness as she inserted her key in the side porch. The hall was dimly-lit, a single light burning on a wall bracket. But the door of the sitting-room was half-open, throwing a lozenge of light on the hall tiles. Kate's relief that Caroline was home turned to surprise as she heard laughter coming from the room. At first she wondered if Mrs Treherne was there with Caroline but then she heard Sarah's voice.

'Thanks ever so much for the game, Aunt Carol. It was super.'

'That's all right, my chick. Now you'd better hurry off to bed. Sleep tight.'

A moment later Sarah, still fully dressed, came hurrying out into the hall. She stopped dead on seeing Kate, a school-girl caught in an act of disobedience. Kate motioned her closer, keeping her voice low.

'What on earth are you doing up at this time of night? You promised me you'd go to bed at eight-thirty.'

Sarah's head was lowered, her voice sullen with guilt. 'Aunt Carol said it didn't matter – that she'd have a game with me.'

'Did you father give you permission to stay up?'

Sarah's chestnut hair swung. 'No,' she muttered. 'He'd already gone out.'

A sudden tap-tap of heels on the hall tiles made Kate turn quickly. Caroline paused a few feet away, a cigarette in her hand. She gave a sharp, hard laugh.

'Hello; you weren't out long. What are you doing – tearing a strip off Sarah for being up a bit later than usual?'

There was danger in her – Kate could sense it. Thinking it safer not to reply she turned to Sarah instead. 'Go straight up to bed now, darling. It's very late and you have to go to school tomorrow.'

There was more contrition than sullenness now in the glance Sarah threw Kate. Caroline saw it and her face hardened. 'Don't look so ashamed, my chick. You've done nothing wrong. If your nanny wants to pick a quarrel with anyone, let her pick it with me.'

Under the simulated amusement the menace was unmistakable. Motioning Sarah to run upstairs Kate followed, her face pale. She was halfway up when Caroline's voice, harsh now that Sarah had gone, halted her like a steel blade at her throat.

'I think I'd like a talk with you, Miss Fielding. Come down here again.'

Kate turned slowly. In some strange way Caroline's very beauty, her blonde, piled-up hair, slim figure, and elegant dress made her more menacing in the dimly-lit hall than a plainer woman would have seemed. Kate thought of a sleek and lovely cat, hungry to sink its claws in an enemy.

She could not keep her voice steady as she regained the hall. 'Yes, Miss Worth. What do you want?'

Caroline's voice was little more than a whisper. 'You've no idea, have you, Miss Fielding? You're such an innocent girl... You weren't trying to make that child feel so ashamed of breaking her promise that she'd turn her resentment against me, were you?'

It was the last accusation Kate had expected and it bewildered her. 'I was angry with her for breaking her promise – of course I was – but I'd no thought of turning her against you. Why should you think that?'

'You answer that yourself, dear,' the menacing voice purred.

Kate's throat was dry. 'I never thought of such a thing. It's hard enough to get Sarah out of bed in the morning at the best of times: it's terribly difficult if she stays up as late as this. But as for trying to turn her against you...'

'You wouldn't dream of doing anything like that... Any more than you'd deliberately stage an affair like the one over the book a week last Sunday. That was purely for John's sake.' The sarcasm in the purring voice was like acid. 'You were only doing your duty there too, weren't you, dear?'

At least this was no surprise... 'That did look bad, I know – that was why I asked you to go outside with me into the corridor. I couldn't help it when Mr Leavengate followed us.'

'It was a nice touch, dear. It almost fooled me until I realised he was certain to think it was John you were trying to avoid and not himself.'

'But why should I do such a thing deliberately? What would the point be?'

Caroline gave a pointed gaze around the hall. Her high-arched brows were raised quizzically when she looked back at Kate. 'Isn't it rather obvious, dear? You're talking to another woman, you know – not a man.'

Until now, feeling the ground beneath her steepening, Kate had been hanging desperately on the brakes. Now, in her resentment, she let go. 'That's not true. I'm employed here to look after the children's interests and that's all I've been doing. You've no right to think every woman is the same...' She broke off on realising the stress she had laid on the word 'every'.

In the semi-darkness Caroline's green eyes were suddenly glowing. 'I heard you, dear – every woman is the same... Go on.'

Kate was clinging to the brakes again although she knew it was now too late. 'I'm only trying to say it isn't fair to suggest I've any ulterior motive for looking after the children. I'm not saying I haven't grown fond of them, but even if I hadn't I'm still employed to protect their interests. And what have I done that's so serious? Asked you not to read from a book that gives John nightmares and told Sarah she oughtn't to break her promises. Is that so terrible?'

'And that's all you've done?' There was a subtle change in the low, purring voice. 'Nothing else, dear?'

It had to come, Kate thought. The rest had been only the softening up before the real attack was launched.

'If you mean my mentioning the boy to Mr Leavengate last night, I couldn't help it. He guessed something was wrong and ordered me to tell him about it.'

'Ordered you!' The words were like a sudden whiplash. 'How could he order you to tell him something he didn't know?'

'He guessed. I can't explain how but he did. I couldn't help it.'

The woman's appearance had changed with her voice, a thinness coming to her lovely face. 'You're lying. You deliberately told him against my express orders. Why?'

There was a frightening feline power about the woman – Kate knew she had to assert herself or be dominated.

'What does it matter? You said yourself the

boy was badly behaved and not important. So why is he so important to you and why can't Mr Leavengate be told about him?'

The effect of her words was uncanny. Caroline's glowing eyes suddenly went blank as if tight shutters had been drawn over them. 'If your prying little mind must know there's a very good reason why I don't want Mr Leavengate ever to meet this boy – it could bring him great unhappiness. So if you care anything about him and his children you'll never mention the boy to anyone in this house again. Does that satisfy your curiosity?'

Kate, bewildered by Caroline's words and change of mood, did not recover herself before the opportunity of questioning had gone. When Caroline, who had walked over to the sitting-room door, turned her voice was threatening again.

'You've resented me ever since I came here – I've known it just as I've known the reason why. That's something I can be amused at – you're only a servant here and no one' her red lips curled as she stressed the words – 'regards you as anything else. But meddling in things you don't understand and are not your concern is something else. My advice to you is to start looking out for another job – you're becoming redundant here in any case. And in the meantime keep your prying self to yourself or you'll regret it. That's something I can promise you.'

Kate went blindly up the stairs. The sudden-
ness of Caroline's attack, its venom, and
then the odd climax suggesting it had
sprung out of concern for Philip, had left
her both numbed and confused. How could
this unknown boy, unknown to Philip or, for
that matter, unknown to any of them except
Sarah, possibly cause Philip unhappiness?
Kate felt an urgent need to know. For if it
were true her opinion of Caroline might
have to be drastically revised.

She went down the corridor to say good
night to Sarah. The girl was already in bed,
her light switched off. As Kate tiptoed
towards the bed a small, ashamed voice
came out of the darkness. 'Is that you, Kate?'

Kate sat on the edge of the bed. 'Yes,
darling. I've just come to say good night.'

A moment of silence followed and then a
hand as small and warm as a bird crept into
her own. 'I'm sorry about the promise, Kate.
But we were having such fun I forgot the
time. And Aunt Carol said it didn't matter
anyway.'

Kate bent down to kiss her. 'It's all right,
darling – it's all over now.'

Two contritious eyes stared up at her. 'Did
you have a quarrel with her, Kate?'

Kate guessed she had heard their voices
rising from the hall. 'A little one, darling,

I'm afraid. But don't worry about it.'

The warm hand gripped tighter. 'I'm ever so sorry. It's all my fault, isn't it?'

Kate knew there would never be a better opportunity and succumbed to an irresistible urge of temptation. 'Darling, there's just one thing I want to ask you before you go to sleep. Did Billy say if he had ever met Aunt Carol or Mrs Treherne before?'

She felt the child's slight involuntary withdrawal and her heart missed a beat. 'I told you yesterday,' Sarah muttered. 'He never saw Aunt Carol – I met her after he'd gone.'

There was the evasion again, transparent in so honest a child. 'But what about Mrs Treherne, darling? Had he met her before?'

The troubled silence was longer this time. 'That was what I wasn't supposed to tell you,' the girl muttered at last.

Kate felt her pulse quicken. 'You mean he'd met Mrs Treherne before and Aunt Carol asked you to keep it a secret?'

Sarah shifted restlessly. 'In a way. But only 'cause I wanted to myself.'

Kate was beginning to understand. 'She told you something against Billy – something you didn't want anyone else to hear?'

Sarah nodded miserably.

'Where had Billy met Mrs Treherne before? Did he tell you?'

Sarah's reply surprised her. 'He hadn't

114

met her – not properly, I mean. He'd just seen her before, that was all. When he was down here during his Christmas holidays.'

Kate's head was whirling. 'Tell me exactly what he did say, darling. Try hard to remember.'

Sarah rose on her elbows, her troubled eyes bright in the darkness. 'When I saw him on Sunday morning he said the woman who'd shooed him from here had been the same woman he'd seen at Christmas. He remembered her because of the funny way she'd been behaving. He'd been playing near the summer house when he saw her and another woman coming along the path from the main road. He said they looked as if they didn't want anyone to see them, and when Mrs Treherne saw him he ran away. But he didn't run far: he hid behind a hedge and saw them go into the summer house. After a while only Mrs Treherne came out and went back to Whitesands.' A sob entered Sarah's voice. 'That's what he told me. I didn't know then he was lying.'

A dozen questions came to Kate's lips but one took priority over them all. 'He said there was another woman with Mrs Treherne. Did he know her or tell you what she looked like?'

'No; he didn't know who she was. Only that she was fair and younger-looking. But it doesn't matter' – Sarah's voice was sullen now with misery – 'because I know now he wasn't telling the truth.'

Somewhere deep inside Kate's mind a heavy stone had fallen, imperilling in some strange way her concept of peaceful Whitesands. She let out her breath slowly. 'How did you find out he wasn't telling the truth, darling?'

'Because of what Aunt Carol told me after I'd seen him on Sunday. She'd found out from Mrs Treherne what had really happened. He'd been stealing things from the summer house and Mrs Treherne had seen him. I didn't believe it at first but Aunt Carol said she'd found out for certain that it was true and if ever the police were to hear of it they'd put him in prison. That's why he hadn't to come back here and why I couldn't tell anyone, even you, Kate.'

For the first time Kate felt she hated Caroline. She pressed the upset girl back on her pillow. 'You needn't worry about it any more, darling. I shan't say anything to anybody and the police won't touch Billy.'

'But they do put people who steal into prison, don't they?'

'Not little boys and girls. And anyway what happened at Christmas is over and won't be brought up again.'

The girl clung to her. 'Oh, I've been so worried, Kate. I know he oughtn't to have stolen things and that I couldn't see him again, but I still didn't want anything to happen to him.'

'Nothing will happen to him – I promise you that. Now try to forget all about it and go to sleep.'

Her reassurances calmed the girl and when she had settled down Kate went back along the corridor to her room. Although the night was warm her body still felt chilled as she undressed and climbed into bed. Lying in the darkness she tried to assemble the newly-given pieces of the jigsaw into some sort of picture but each time a single thought scattered them like a brutal hand. If she were to believe Billy's version of what happened – and all she had heard so far made her feel it was the true one – then Mrs Treherne had furtively taken a younger, blonde woman to hide in the summer house over the Christmas weekend. *And it had been during that weekend that Elizabeth Leavengate had fallen from the great Whitesands headland to her death.*

Lying there, colder with fear than at any time she could remember, Kate suddenly heard light footsteps in the corridor outside. Bolt upright now, she listened. They appeared to pass into Sarah's room and a moment later she heard low voices.

With her mind a turmoil of fear Kate almost leapt from her bed and ran into the girl's room. She was checked by the sceptic in her – the civilised woman that was as yet unconvinced that danger could exist in a respectable country house in peaceful England. Caroline had talked alone to Sarah dozens of times before – what danger could there be now?

Yet it was a tremendous relief when the voices died away and the sharp, light footsteps returned along the corridor. It was only then, so intense had Kate's concern been for the girl, that she realised what Caroline had been asking her…

It brought back fear to her, a personal fear this time, as the footsteps stopped in the corridor and her door swung open.

6

The switch at the door clicked down and the sudden flood of light struck Kate like a blow. Bolt upright in bed she saw Caroline close the door and turn towards her. The mask had dropped from the woman's lovely face now, it was thin and vicious as she moved menacingly to the foot of the bed.

'You dared to question Sarah – not five minutes after my warning to you downstairs... You insolent prying little bitch.'

The insult and the viciousness of its delivery choked off Kate's protests like a hand at her throat. Frozen she watched the fury blazing in the woman's green eyes.

'I ordered you never to mention the boy's name in the house again. And straight away you come upstairs and talk about him to Sarah. Why? Tell me why?'

Kate found her voice. 'I don't understand why there is such a mystery over him and why he mustn't meet Mr Leavengate.'

The thinned red lips twisted in contempt and aversion. 'You meddling fool – of course you can't understand.'

Sitting there in bed and dressed only in her pyjamas gave Kate a feeling or being unprotected. 'Why am I a fool? I don't like Sarah to be alienated from me. She's always trusted me before and you must have known I would never get a boy of eleven into trouble with the police.' Recovering a little from the shock of Caroline's entry she realised again the need to fight back if the woman was not to dominate her will. 'That story you told Sarah wasn't the real reason you wanted her to keep quiet. It couldn't have been, after what you said to me downstairs.'

She did not know quite what to expect but felt certain at least of another outbreak of fury. Instead, although Caroline's eyes glowed ominously, her expression did not change.

'So you've managed to work that out, have you? You must feel proud of yourself.'

Kate had expected anything but this admission. Her skin prickled and she had to brace herself to avoid shrinking back as Caroline threw a glance at the closed door and then approached her bedside. She spoke in a low, bitter voice.

'It's obvious enough you're going to go on prying if you don't hear the real reason. So I've no choice but to tell it to you. But if after that you as much as mention the boy's name in these parts I'll make you wish you'd never been born. Is that clearly understood?'

Kate could do nothing but nod her head and wait. Caroline sat on the edge of the bed, a gesture deprived of all familiarity by the thinness of her face. She took a cigarette, snapped a lighter, and then turned her feline eyes on Kate.

'That melodramatic mind of yours has got the idea there is a mystery here at Whitesands in which Mrs Treherne and I are involved. Well, there is, but it's a very different kind of mystery from the schoolgirlish ideas you've got. It's a mystery that neither Mrs Treherne nor myself want Mr Leavengate to hear about or it'll nearly break his heart.'

In the hushed moment of silence that followed Kate heard the chiming of a clock downstairs. Something tapped against the window, a bat or insect. Then Caroline's voice came again.

'It all started about the middle of last year. I was in Rome when I got an unexpected letter from Mrs Treherne. She wanted my advice on a crisis that had developed here.' Caroline paused, blew jets of smoke through her nostrils, and then turned her eyes fully on Kate. 'To be brief about it she'd discovered that Elizabeth Leavengate was having an affair with a man from St Marks.'

To Kate it was news as unexpected and brutal as a sudden gunshot. 'An affair ... Mrs Leavengate? But I always thought they'd been a very happy couple.'

Caroline's face twisted cynically. 'I wasn't aware you knew anything about them,

121

having only come here after her death.'

'I don't know first-hand, of course. But everyone says they were devoted. And Mr Leavengate was so terribly upset – it was months before he recovered...' Her voice trailed off at Caroline's expression.

'Don't you understand – he never found out! And if you listen you'll understand why. From what Mrs Treherne told me in her letter Elizabeth had been acting queerly for months. For days on end she would be too tired to move from her bed and then she would get an unnatural attack of energy when no one, not even her doctors, could keep her in her room. Mrs Treherne had noticed these feverish attacks often came in the evenings when Philip was working late. She used to go for long walks along the cliffs and would never allow anyone to accompany her, but one night, worrying in case she had an accident, Mrs Treherne followed her and saw her turn off the cliff path to the summer house. As she approached it a man came to the door and they both went inside. And it was over two hours before Elizabeth came out alone and returned to Whitesands.'

Kate could not hold back her protest. 'But what right had Mrs Treherne, a house-keeper, to spy on her like that? And why did she write letters about it?'

Lightning fast, Caroline was immediately under her guard. 'I'd forgotten – you're the type that wouldn't pry on anyone, aren't you? She had every right. Philip himself had asked her to keep an eye on Elizabeth when he was out – he knew her mind was affected by this time. That was why Mrs Treherne was so upset by this discovery – the last thing she wanted to do was to tell Philip and yet at the same time she realised Elizabeth had to be protected both from herself and this man. There was the danger he might be an adventurer playing on her unbalanced mind for his own ends. On the other hand, if his affections were genuine and Elizabeth had managed to keep from him the dangerous state of her health, he might not realise the risks of getting her into an emotional entanglement. Either way there was danger and Mrs Treherne – who, in spite of your opinion, is an extremely loyal and conscientious woman – felt it was her responsibility to try to save Elizabeth from herself. That was the reason she wrote to me – there was no one else she dared go to for advice.'

Caroline paused, pulled on her cigarette. 'If it had been possible I should have come straight here. As it wasn't I wrote and told Mrs Treherne to meet this man and make certain he knew about Elizabeth's condition. A few weeks later I had a second letter telling me she had forced a meeting on him but that he denied everything. He was a married man, she had discovered, living in St Marks.

As it was clear from Elizabeth's behaviour the affair was still going on, Mrs Treherne had then gone to her, admitted she knew everything, and begged her for Philip's sake to stop the meetings herself.

'Elizabeth broke down and admitted everything. Mrs Treherne said she felt very sorry for her – it was obvious she was completely dominated by this man. At the same time she was cunning: she knew Mrs Treherne wouldn't betray her and so went on meeting him. When I heard this I knew something desperate had to be done if Philip wasn't to get wind of it and so I told Mrs Treherne to try to contact the man's wife. This took her a long time but she finally managed it. At first the woman wouldn't believe her but at last Mrs Treherne persuaded her to go to the summer house. Her husband had left a few incriminating things there – a scarf, I think, and similar trifles. Nothing that could prove infidelity, of course, but that didn't matter. They convinced the woman her husband had been going to the summer house when he had told her he was going to his club, and from her tone it was clear he wouldn't deceive her again.'

The question came out before Kate could check it. 'Was she a fair woman? Younger, of course, than Mrs Treherne?'

Caroline's green eyes caught the lamplight and she nodded. 'So you're beginning to understand at last, are you? It was Christmas now – all this had taken a long time – and Mrs Treherne noticed this boy Billy when she was taking the woman to the summer house. If she had ignored him he probably wouldn't have paid any attention to either of them. But in her anxiety she was nervous and shooed him away, only to notice him later spying on them from behind a hedge. So you can imagine how she felt when she saw Sarah bringing him to the house – her first thought was to get him off the estate as quickly as possible. Do I have to explain why or are you able to see now why I don't ever want Philip to meet him?'

Kate cleared her throat. 'Of course I see.'

Caroline's unblinking gaze did not leave her. 'You might argue the chances of anything coming out are small… If you were right I still wouldn't take them. But I don't know they are so small. Children chatter and Philip's shrewd – he doesn't need much evidence to build up a case. And I also don't know what happened between him and Elizabeth during those last few months – it might even be possible he had a suspicion something was wrong. So I'm playing it safe, treating that boy as if he were dynamite and keeping him as far from us all and Whitesands as I can. I think too much of Philip to do anything else.'

Kate was remembering what Wirral had

told her about hearing Philip and Elizabeth quarrelling in the last few weeks before Elizabeth death and could not fault the woman's logic. 'So it wasn't true what you told Sarah about Billy – he hadn't been seen by Mrs Treherne stealing things from the summer house?'

Caroline's slim shoulders lifted contemptuously. 'Of course he hadn't. But I had to do something to stop her seeing him and chattering about him. Just as I had to divert Philip's interest in him when you started your meddling.'

There was still one thing she had not explained. One all-important thing. Without knowing why Kate found her muscles were tensed again. 'But it was this same weekend that Mrs Leavengate died. What happened to her?'

Caroline looked down at her cigarette, saw it was burned down to a stub and looked around for an ashtray. Finally she ground it out on the tiles before the electric heater. She lit another before turning back to Kate. Her expression was twisted, half-rueful. 'She fell four hundred feet from Whitesands Cliffs. You must know that.'

'I do. But why? Surely there must be some connection with all you've told me.'

'Perhaps there was.' Kate thought there was a trace of defiance in her voice now. 'She had an assignment for the Saturday evening – Philip was attending some club function in Exeter. As naturally the man wouldn't have been able to turn up she would be upset...' She finished the sentence with another shrug of her shoulders.

'You think in her disappointment she might have committed suicide?'

'It's just possible, I suppose. As I say, her mind wasn't normal.'

'But then was it wise to do all this? Wasn't there a less risky way?'

Dislike blazed again in Caroline's eyes. 'What other way was there? Let Philip know what was going on? Let loose a scandal that might have ruined him professionally? If I'd been here I might have been able to handle things more tactfully but as I wasn't there was no other way. After all' – inhaling smoke deeply again – 'she had no one to blame but herself. And who can know what the reason was, anyway? It was almost certainly an accident – Mrs Treherne says there was a devil of a gale blowing that night.'

She was defending herself now, Kate thought, wondering for the first time if her reason for keeping Elizabeth's infidelity from Philip was wholly altruistic. Had she a fear he might bitterly resent the advice she had given Mrs Treherne? Was he the kind of man who would risk his wife's death to terminate her infidelity? Kate thought he was not.

And yet she could see clearly enough he

127

must never be told. To give him the twin shock of learning that the woman he had loved had committed both adultery and suicide was unthinkable. In this, at least, she and Caroline could be allies.

Caroline had moved to the bed foot and was staring at her with hard condemning eyes. 'I hope you see now the damage your meddling could have done. Whatever Elizabeth's guilt she was my cousin, she's dead, and I'm not having her name tainted with scandal. Nor am I going to have Phil broken-hearted. So from now on keep your prying nose out of things?'

'What about Mrs Treherne? And the man and woman? Isn't there a danger of them talking?'

'Mrs Treherne has promised me never to mention the affair to a soul, and she won't. As for the man and woman' – Caroline's lips were a thin, menacing line – 'they know better than to talk. I've seen to that.'

She walked to the door. Before opening it she turned. 'Remember – you don't say a word of this to anybody. And that includes your father, mother and boy friend. If you do I'll have you in court for slander before you know what's hit you. You'll have no witnesses to support your case and I'll see you get what you deserve. Now get your meddling head down and go to sleep.'

Darkness swooped on Kate as the light

switch clicked off. Still sitting upright, the bedclothes huddled around her, she heard Caroline's light, sharp footsteps recede and vanish down the corridor.

It was a full minute before Kate lay back, noticing for the first time how cramped her muscles had become under the tension of the last fifteen minutes. Lying there in the darkness, freed from the tyranny of Caroline's presence, she tried to integrate all her earlier disjointed fragments of knowledge with the story she had just been told.

Everything seemed to fit and make a complete picture. Elizabeth's strange fevers and mysterious long walks along the cliffs when Philip was working late were now fully explained. So was Mrs Treherne's peremptory dismissal of Billy from Whitesands – it was exactly the thing a blunt unsubtle woman like the housekeeper would do in such circumstances. It made Caroline's fictitious story about Billy to Sarah understandable, if not commendable, and explained the strange intimacy between her and Mrs Treherne which had been the very backbone of the mystery. It cleared up the identity of the fair woman Billy had seen going to the summer house with the housekeeper and explained their apparent furtiveness. It even offered a plausible explanation for Elizabeth Leavengate's death, for it was surely quite possible that the woman, feverish and neurotic from her disease, had thrown herself from the cliffs on discovering her lover had deserted her.

With her conscious mind satisfied the mystery was laid Kate tried to relax. It was only then, when her tensed nerves refused to slacken, that she realised a deeper, more intuitive part of her mind was not satisfied. It could not offer her a flaw in Caroline's story on which to base its incredulity – it seemed there was none – but instead it gave her flashbacks of memory. The odd gleam in Caroline's eyes on being asked if the man's wife had been fair-haired. Had it been the lamplight or could it have been triumph? And the way her skin had prickled on Caroline's approach to her bedside. Kate could feel it again as she lay there … as though a primeval instinct had warned her of the approach of evil. She tried to dismiss the thought as melodramatic but knew nevertheless that Caroline had always given her an awareness of evil.

It was then she understood why her intuition had so stubbornly rejected Caroline's story. Not on rational grounds – it stood up impregnably to argument – but because it was out of character. Caroline was ruthless and determined to marry Philip – of that Kate was certain. Then why had she made this positive effort to save Elizabeth – the woman who had stolen

Philip from her thirteen years ago – when all she need have done was sit back and wait for the rupture that must surely have come sooner or later between her and Philip? And why was she suppressing her knowledge of Elizabeth's infidelity now when by releasing it she might assist her chances of success?

Once released, Kate's doubts were like tiny ferrets, running amok inside her head and tearing her relief to shreds. More memories came to her. The clever way Caroline had used facts before as props to her lies. The almost brutal way she had broken the news of Elizabeth's infidelity: there had seemed more enjoyment in that than regret. And her admission that Elizabeth might have committed suicide because of the action taken against her. At the time it had surprised Kate. Now she wondered if it had not been used to add the final brilliant gloss of credulity to the story.

Then, in time for Kate to avoid facing the consequence of her suspicions, reaction drove them back. In this new castigated mood she did not spare herself. She was a woman and she did not like Caroline – could not prejudice be behind most of her doubts? The fact Caroline was now throwing a very large hook after Philip did not necessarily mean she would not have tried to help her cousin when she was alive: the two things could be quite separate. And if her story were not true, then why had Elizabeth kept taking those wild, feverish walks towards the summer house when Philip was absent? If Caroline were lying – and here Kate's mind neatly side-stepped the implications if she were – she could still hardly have been certain that Elizabeth would choose that particular Saturday night to take one of those walks.

It seemed impossible the story could be false. Because if it were... Again Kate's mind leapt away, like a horse seeing a crouching wolf. Her mind, searching for a distraction, heard the sound of a car in the drive outside and fixed on it in relief. She heard the faint crunch of Philip's footsteps on the gravel, the muffled slam of the garage doors, and his footsteps again on the tiled floor of the hall below. Then, after a few minutes, sounds at the other end of the corridor as he went to his room.

And then silence again and a resumption of the torture. A fair-haired woman going with Mrs Treherne to the summer house... Everything depended on who that woman was – she made herself face that one issue. If it were not Caroline, she need worry no more. But if it was Caroline – what would that mean...?

She found her body was moist with sweat and knew she would never rest until she knew the truth. And for that she needed

Billy, the only person in the world who could help. How to make contact with him and what the outcome of that contact might be were thoughts that kept her tossing restlessly far into the night.

The following morning, while waiting in the side porch for Philip to drive out of the garage, Sarah asked Kate about the previous night. Kate was not surprised; she had half-expected the girl to come to her bedroom after Caroline had left it. The diffidence of Sarah's tone and expression made it obvious she was worrying that she might have betrayed Kate's confidence.

'I couldn't help telling Aunt Caroline last night that you'd been asking me more about Billy and that I'd told you everything. Did it matter, Kate? I heard her go to your room afterwards.'

Kate threw a quick glance at the corridor behind them. It was empty. She forced a smile as she turned back to the girl. 'No; it didn't matter a bit, darling. Don't worry about it.'

Sarah's worried expression showed she was not convinced. 'I thought it sounded as if you were quarrelling again. Were you, Kate?'

Although Kate knew she would have to talk to Sarah about Billy again, she was desperately anxious to keep the girl free from any involvement in the affair and from any conflict of loyalties between herself and Caroline. Relieved to see the car draw up alongside the porch at that moment she shook her head. 'We'll talk about it when we've more time, darling, but there's nothing to worry about. Nothing whatever, so forget all about it. Off you go to school now and see you enjoy the film tonight.'

Kate was aware of a subtle change in the atmosphere of Whitesands that day. It was as though the house had suddenly grown a thousand eyes and each one was following her. She could not put a finger on anything tangible, and yet wherever she went she felt under observation. Inside the house she felt ears were listening. Outside, in the garden, she felt eyes watching her from Whitesands' many windows, and yet when she turned sharply, as she did more than once that day, the same windows were blank and expressionless in the late June sunlight.

She had no opportunity of speaking to Sarah that day. Philip had arranged to meet the girl on her leaving school, take her to tea in St Marks, and afterwards to a film show. He had invited Kate to accompany them, but knowing Caroline was joining them she had declined on the pretext of not liking the main star in the film. An important factor in Kate's decision was her reluctance to leave John alone with Mrs Treherne. For although the boy did not have the same fear of the housekeeper as Sarah, Kate was determined to do her best to prevent the children being left alone with either her or Caroline until her fears were resolved one way or the other.

Her first real opportunity to speak to Sarah about Billy came just before dinner on Wednesday evening. She was in the tool shed alongside the garages, putting away John's tricycle, when she heard the crunch of tyres on the gravel drive. Guessing it was Sarah returning from a visit to her friends Kate kept out of sight in the shed. A moment later Sarah, boyish in shorts and a round-necked shirt, steered her bicycle through the half-open door. Thrusting it unceremoniously against a workbench she would have run out without seeing Kate if Kate had not checked her.

'Darling, just a minute. There's something I want to ask you.'

Sarah spun round, her bright eyes curious in the shadows. 'Hello, Kate. I didn't see you. What's the matter?'

As casually as she could Kate pulled the door closed. Then she turned with a smile on the puzzled girl. 'I want to talk to you about Billy again, darling. I want you to do me a favour.'

'Billy!' At the mention of the boy's name Sarah's curiosity jumped like the mercury in a sphygmomanometer. 'What sort of favour?'

Kate was anxiously aware that her curiosity

had to be brought down, for it was vital she spoke to nobody. 'Nothing very exciting, I'm afraid. I just want you to let me know if you see him again. Will you do that for me?'

Sarah looked puzzled now. 'But I'm not seeing him any more. You know why – I told you.'

Hating what she was doing but knowing there was no other way, Kate went on: 'I'm not going to get him into any trouble, darling, if that's what you're afraid of. It's just the opposite, in fact. I've been thinking about it and wondering if it's just possible Mrs Treherne was wrong in thinking he was taking things from the summer house. He might just have been curious, taken a look inside, and then run away when he saw her. After all, none of us has ever heard this story, have we?'

A worried frown puckered Sarah's oval face. 'Aunt Carol seems pretty certain she was right. And daddy told me not to play with him any more.'

Kate did not miss this opportunity. 'That's the very reason I want you to keep all this a secret between the two of us. They might all be right and then we'd look pretty silly, wouldn't we?' She laid a hand on the girl's warm, chestnut hair. 'I'm not asking you to disobey your daddy, darling. All I want you to do, if you see Billy around here again, is ask him to wait where he is and come straight and tell me. Then I'll go and talk to him. If it seems that Mrs Treherne is right, then of course you mustn't see him again. But if he has a reasonable explanation it might be different, mightn't it?'

Sarah's face had been growing steadily brighter and brighter. 'Do you really believe he might not have been stealing at all?'

'I don't know, darling. But I think we ought to give him a chance to explain.'

Sarah's voice became shrill with excitement. 'If he hadn't been, he could come here and play then, couldn't he?'

Kate put her fingers to her lips. 'Ssh, darling; we don't want anyone else to know. Do you think he's likely to come back to Cornwall for his summer holidays?'

The girl's face dropped in disappointment. 'That's the trouble. He wasn't very sure before. And now he might not want to. Oh, Kate; why didn't you think of this before? I'm sure you're right – Mrs Treherne is always thinking nasty things about people.'

Kate's whole body was tensed in her effort to hush the girl's chatter without making the depth of her anxiety too obvious. 'Keep calm, darling. We don't know he is innocent yet – that's what we're going to try to find out. Do you know the address of his relatives in St Marks?'

Sarah shook her head unhappily.

'Then do you know his home address in

Bristol?' Kate bit her lip as again the girl shook her head. 'Then we'll just have to hope he comes round here again, darling, or that you run into him in St Marks.'

Sarah's face suddenly brightened. 'The little park in St Marks. I remember now. He told me he often plays in there because of the pond – he sails his boats in it.'

Kate felt her heart quicken again. 'All right, darling – perhaps during the summer holidays you and I will go there once or twice to look for him. But remember, in the meantime you're not to say a word to anyone. If you don't promise I shan't go and look for him.'

The girl's response was heartfelt. 'I promise, Kate. Cross my heart.'

'Good. Now run along inside and wash. It's almost time for dinner.'

She pushed the shed door open and Sarah scuttled out and ran into the house. Kate's eyes searched the drive anxiously as she followed, but she saw no one. It was only when she reached the side porch, from which the side of the shed was visible, that she noticed Mrs Treherne was standing there, emptying a swill bucket into one of the three huge dustbins that stood alongside the shed. Her back was to Kate and she gave no sign of noticing her, clumping the bucket vigorously on the bin top to empty it before turning back out of sight towards one of the rear doors that led to the kitchen.

Kate felt numb as she went into the house. The walls of the shed were wooden and thin: the housekeeper could hardly have missed overhearing their conversation unless she had only just gone out. Certainly, if she had heard Kate's instructions to Sarah, Caroline would hear of them before the day was out.

And what would happen then? Suddenly Kate stopped dead in her tracks. Billy presented no threat to Caroline's story until he was identified and asked to give witness. *And he could only be identified by Sarah.* Therefore, if the wild suspicions that had tormented her throughout Monday night had any substance, she might have put the girl in terrible danger. She tried to thrust the thought away as fantastic, but it haunted her for the rest of the day like a grey, hideous spectre.

7

But suspicions, however intense, are like people, they need food to keep them alive. Kate discovered this in the week that followed. It was uneventful, as were the first five days of the week following it. It was mid-summer now at Whitesands, the long days warm and sunny and the massed flowers of the gardens in their full glory. With the familiar domestic routine following day after day – Sarah going off to school, John playing outside in the sunshine, Mrs Treherne rattling cooking utensils in the kitchen – a reaction set in Kate that made it more and more difficult to keep the worst of her suspicions alive. Caroline might be calculating, she might be ambitious to become the mistress of Whitesands, she certainly disliked Kate intensely: but none of these things need mean she had been involved in Elizabeth's death. Nor (and each day the thought seemed more bizarre) did they mean Sarah was in any danger from her, although the school holidays were now little more than two weeks away.

The effect of this reaction was to make Kate feel a certain shame and diffidence towards Caroline on the few occasions when they met alone. And the very insolence with which Caroline accepted her discomposure seemed to strengthen further the claims of her story.

It was in this new mood that Kate sat at dinner with Philip, Caroline and Sarah one Friday night. Coffee had just been served when Mrs Treherne returned to the dining-room. Her dour black eyes fixed themselves on Kate.

'Mr Marsden's here and wants to see you, miss. I've shown him into the library.'

As Kate put aside her napkin and rose Philip turned to her. 'Finish your coffee, Kate. He oughtn't to come when you're having dinner.'

'I have finished,' she told him, glad as always of an excuse to get away from Caroline. 'You will excuse me, won't you?'

He shrugged. 'Of course. But tell him not to come at this time again.'

Kate knew the purpose of Marsden's visit – every Friday he helped her draw up the graph of the cattle experiment. As she entered the library he rose ponderously from one of the hide armchairs, a plump friendly man with a florid face and a hearty Cornish voice.

'Sorry if I've upset your dinner, Miss Kate. But my missus wants to go to the pictures tonight, so I had to come a bit earlier than usual.'

'It's all right,' Kate assured him, going over to the desk and pulling out the pile of returns. 'The experiment ends next weekend, doesn't it?'

'That's right, miss. And going well it is, too.' He handed her a folded piece of paper. 'Here's today's return – the best yet, I think.'

Kate took it from him and laid it on the desk. Then she began paging through the papers, taking out the current week's returns. 'There's yesterday's. And Wednesday's...' Her voice suddenly broke off.

Marsden glanced at her curiously. 'What's the matter, miss?'

Kate began paging through the top sheets again. Her face was puzzled. 'That's strange. The returns for Sunday, Monday and Tuesday appear to be missing.'

Marsden stood over her awkwardly while she searched right through the pile of papers. Her eyes were wide with alarm when she glanced up at him again. 'They're not here. They've gone.'

'Are you certain you put 'em in there, miss? You didn't maybe put 'em in another drawer?'

Kate's headshake was positive. 'I always file away each day's return as soon as you give it to me.'

'Then maybe they've slipped off and are among the other papers in the drawer.'

Kate searched all three drawers thoroughly,

taking each out in turn to ensure the papers had not slipped behind them. When she finished her face was pale. 'They're definitely not here.'

Marsden was looking uncomfortable now. 'I know I gave 'em to you, miss. I've been extra careful, knowing Mr Leavengate's been doing the experiment for one of his friends.'

'I know that. I'm not blaming you.'

'Mightn't it be the children, miss,' Marsden asked, relieved. 'There's no lock on the drawer – maybe one of 'em wanted some paper and took a few sheets, not knowing what they were.'

Kate shook her head. 'Neither of them would touch the desk. They both know all the papers in it are business papers.'

As she spoke a sudden vision leapt into her mind like a bright film on a screen. Caroline standing over the graph … asking the importance of each day's return … taking all other secretarial work from her but leaving that single important task…

'What is it, miss?' Marsden had to speak twice to Kate before she heard him. 'You're as white as a sheet.'

Kate turned sharply away. 'Nothing … I'm just worried, that's all. I know how much Mr Leavengate wanted it to be success for his friend's sake.'

Her distress brought Marsden's good nature to the surface. 'They can't be far away, miss – it don't make sense. I'll tell you what – I'll go and tell the missus what's happened and then I'll come back and we'll have a good scout around before we say anything to Mr Leavengate. What d'you say?'

Her voice had a dull, flat sound. 'I don't think it'll be any use. I know I put them in the drawer – if they've gone they won't be anywhere else in the house.'

Marsden's puzzlement grew. 'But if you're sure of that, it can only mean someone's taken 'em... Wait a minute – what about Mr Leavengate? Maybe he's borrowed 'em for some reason or other.'

Hope touched Kate, then was gone again. He would have mentioned the returns at the dinner table; he had known Marsden's reason for coming... At that moment she heard firm footsteps cross the tiled hall outside. A vein in her temple began throbbing. The door opened and Philip appeared. He approached them with a smile.

'Have you got it worked out yet? Are things still improving?'

His question was directed at Marsden who was too slow to realise at once the implications of it. 'No, sir. We've three returns short this week and we're wonderin' if you've borrowed them.'

Philip's handsome face turned puzzled. 'Three returns short! I don't follow you.'

Marsden, realising now his guess was

wrong, threw a dismayed glance at Kate. She answered for him. 'Sunday, Monday and Tuesday's returns are missing, Mr Leavengate. I've turned the desk right out but I can't find them anywhere.'

His dark eyebrows came together as he glanced back at Marsden. 'What does that mean? That you didn't take the figures out?'

Kate intervened again, explaining what had happened. His frown deepened. 'I'm not following *you* now, Kate. If you definitely put them into the drawer they could only vanish if someone took them. And who would do that?'

Caroline, she wanted to cry out… So that you'll lose your confidence in me… But she knew that was what Caroline wanted more than anything else…

'I don't know,' she said quietly, eyes lowered. 'All I can tell you is that I've always been most careful to put them away safely. I know how important the experiment is to you.'

He made a sharp exclamation. 'Important! Jack has already told the Agricultural Board how well things are going. He's going to look a damned fool if he can't back up his words in a fortnight's time.'

He strode over to the desk and paged quickly through the pile of returns while Kate and Marsden watched in silence. After pulling the drawer right out he glanced

146

sharply up at Kate.

'You're absolutely sure of this, Kate? You put them in here every evening?'

Her face felt still as she nodded. 'I'm quite sure. I've never missed a day.'

He went to the door. 'All right – then it can only mean someone in the house has taken them, only God knows why. Wait here. I'm going to question the others.'

He returned five minutes later. 'I've asked Caroline, Mrs Treherne, Wirral and Sarah – I've even woken John up – and they all say they've never been near the drawer. In fact, apart from Carol, they say they knew nothing about them. That leaves only the charwomen – have you ever caught any of them opening drawers before?'

Kate shook her head silently.

'Then where can they be, Kate?' His voice was irritable now. 'Confound it – they couldn't have walked away.'

Marsden made a brave attempt to aid Kate. 'Does it matter so much, sir? We've already shown a steady increase for nearly four weeks.'

Philip turned on him sharply. 'Of course it matters, man. You know what these Boards are like – someone's certain to argue these three returns were deliberately lost because the milk yield dropped again. You never thought of keeping copies of your figures, I suppose.' When Marsden shook his head he

147

turned away in disgust. 'That's it, then. Unless they turn up before the next weekend the experiment's a washout.'

A brief, unhappy silence followed as he stared moodily through the library windows, hands clasped behind his back. When he spoke he did not turn around.

'I'll have a word with the charwomen when they come in tomorrow morning. And in the meantime, Kate, I'd like you to make certain they're not lying around anywhere. Even if you feel sure they're not, please look carefully.'

Kate went out silently, followed by the embarrassed Marsden. Her one thought was to reach her room but as she crossed the landing upstairs a door opened and Caroline stepped out.

'Well,' she drawled. 'Have the returns come to light yet?'

Kate had not known whether she would accuse Caroline or not – she had been too distressed to consider it. But now, hearing the mockery behind the question, her bitterness leapt out like the scalding water from a kettle.

'They're not likely to come to light, are they, Miss Worth? You should know better than that.'

Caroline's high-arched eyebrows lifted, more in amusement, than surprise. 'What on earth are you talking about, girl?'

'You knew the importance of that experiment – you asked me everything about it carefully enough. I wondered then why you left it with me when you took all the other work away. Now I know.'

'Really, dear...' The low amused voice was infinitely taunting. 'Then why didn't you tell Mr Leavengate? I'm sure he'd have been most interested.'

'How do you know I didn't?' Kate asked bitterly. 'Because you were listening outside the door?' Her voice ran on, reckless now. 'You're despicable. And one day Mr Leavengate is going to find it out for himself.'

Caroline had darted a swift glance down the empty corridor. Her low laugh mocked Kate as she turned back. 'Never mind, dear. It's not likely you'll be here when it happens, is it?'

For a moment their eyes locked, green eyes cruel with amusement, brown eyes swollen with tears and resentment. Then, with a contemptuous swing of her body and another low laugh Caroline made for the stairs. A grandfather clock on the landing, winding itself up to strike, sounded like an asthmatical man releasing his breath at the break in the tension. Kate went blindly to her room.

Later, when Kate was saying good night to Sarah, she caught sight of Philip and

Caroline from the girl's bedroom window, walking up the front drive. It was a mellow summer evening, with the sun low on the horizon and throwing long shadows across the front lawn. Philip still looked pre-occupied but everything about Caroline, her expression as well as the intimate way she was holding his arm, told Kate she was offering him sympathy. As she watched they strolled through the open front gates and turned down the path that led eastwards across the estate.

Sarah's inquisitive voice made Kate start in confusion. 'What's the matter, Kate? What are you looking at?'

Before Kate could draw the curtains Sarah was out of bed and peering through the window. Kate was profoundly grateful the high bramble bushes that flanked the path were now hiding Philip and Caroline from sight. Sarah was already on the fringe of adolescence and the danger of her making a shrewd guess at the cause of her attention was too embarrassing to contemplate.

Sarah looked puzzled. 'What was it, Kate? You were looking ever so miserable.'

Kate led her back to bed, held her tightly for a moment. She smelt of bath salts and was warm and intensely precious. 'Nothing, darling,' she whispered. 'I was just thinking thoughts, that was all.'

Sarah's arms clung around her neck.

'What sort of thoughts, Kate?'

'Silly thoughts, darling. Not worth talking about. Now go to sleep or you'll have dark circles under your eyes tomorrow.'

As she reached the door Sarah's voice checked her. 'Kate, you weren't thinking you'd like to go back to London – you're not getting tired of being here, are you?'

The tremor of anxiety in the child's usually happy voice caught at Kate's throat. 'Of course I'm not, darling. I wasn't thinking anything like that. Go to sleep and don't think such silly things.'

The children needed her, she knew that. And with Caroline at Whitesands they needed her even more... Yet how much longer could she hold on? Her steps were heavy as she left the bedroom and walked down the long, shadowy corridor.

The following morning Philip called Kate into his study. She had to brace herself before going in. 'Yes, Mr Leavengate?'

He glanced up, then his eyes dropped again on some papers on the desk before him. 'Kate; I need some forms and stationery from the printers for some documents I'm preparing today – I'd like you to take the car and collect them for me. Here's the list. The printers are Martins in Bank Street.'

'Shall I leave John or take him with me?' she asked. 'Sarah's all right – she's gone over to play with the Dundas children.'

He hesitated. 'I'll be here all the morning and I don't think Carol's going out. You can leave him here, I think.'

She took the car keys and the list from him. 'Is there anything else you want while I'm in town?'

The ache inside her grew as she noticed the over-attentiveness he was paying the papers on his desk. 'No thanks, Kate. That's all.'

As she went to the door she felt his eyes lift and follow her. She braced herself again.

'I take it you've had no further luck with the returns?'

'No,' she said quietly, turning. 'No luck at all.'

He seemed about to speak, then gave a quick, impatient shake of his head. 'That's it, then. The charwomen say they know nothing about them. I'll give Jack a ring today... By the way, be as quick as you can with that stuff, will you? I can't finish this job until I get it.'

Out in the hall her misery was like physical pain – if he had openly reprimanded her she would have found it easier to bear. But his quiet, hurt acceptance of her guilt was worse than a hundred angry words and she knew that if it had not been for the children, pain alone would have forced her resignation.

Because John had gone into his playroom and she first wanted to tell him where she was going, Kate left the house by one of the rear doors. As she made her way towards the garages she heard the sound of low voices coming from somewhere down the garden. Although too distant and too low-pitched for the conversation to be distinguishable, the voices had a discordant note that made Kate pause and listen. They belonged to Caroline and Mrs Treherne and Kate's mind instantly flew back to the first Sunday of Caroline's arrival at Whitesands when Kate had seen her and Mrs Treherne having a mysterious argument at the foot of the garden. This time the two women were screened from her by bushes, and even as she listened their voices ceased. Realising they must have caught the sound of her footsteps on the gravel apron behind the house Kate went on hastily and entered the garages.

She waited inside them for a full minute but when no one passed on the way to the house she realised the women were waiting for the car to pull away. As she drove out of the garages she wondered what the reason for the occasional secret discord between them could be. There seemed no cause for it if Caroline's story about Elizabeth were true, and even if it were false Kate could think of nothing that could make a woman like Caroline quarrel on apparently equal terms with a housekeeper.

She was still puzzling about it when she

reached St Marks twenty minutes later. When she arrived at the printers the forms Philip had ordered were not ready and it was after eleven o'clock before she started back. As she turned right at the small hamlet on the cliff road and swung round a bend she was surprised to see Mrs Treherne standing at the roadside. Dour-faced in her uncompromising black dress, there was nevertheless something apprehensive about her as she stared westwards across the cliff. She gave a start on seeing the car, an odd mixture of sullenness and relief entering her expression as she turned to face it.

Kate drew up alongside her. 'Do you want a lift back to the house?'

The woman hesitated. 'Thank you, miss. But I'm out looking for Sarah.'

Kate eyed her curiously. Her dour face seemed active with a strange fear which dislike and caution were holding in a kind of uneasy suspension.

'Sarah? But she went in the opposite direction this morning – over to Dr Dundas's house.'

The housekeeper shook her head. 'No, miss. She had to come back half an hour ago – the doctor was taking Mary and Betty into town. She was at a loose end – maybe that was why Miss Caroline took a walk with her.'

Something indefinable in the woman's voice made Kate suddenly feel cold. 'A walk?

Where have they gone? Along the cliffs?'

For a fraction of a second Mrs Treherne's small eyes met Kate's own. What was that in them – a warning…? Then they were looking away, sullen and infinitely wary again.

'Yes, miss. Apparently Miss Caroline hadn't been to the old watchtower yet and wanted Sarah to take her to it. John told me a few minutes ago.'

'But then what is it, Mrs Treherne? Why have you run out after them?'

The housekeeper's small averted eyes seemed to contract and cover themselves with a black, impenetrable shell of caution. 'I came out because Mr Leavengate asked me where Sarah had gone. I took it he wants to speak to her.'

It sounded thin; it did not fit the woman's uneasiness. Kate pulled the car on to the grass verge and switched off the engine. She jumped out.

'You say Mr Leavengate wants Sarah? I'll go and tell her for you.'

Although Mrs Treherne was gazing across the cliffs Kate imagined she saw a look of relief flit across her swarthy face. Kate was turning away when she remembered and ran back to the car. Pulling out a parcel she thrust it at the housekeeper. 'Please give that to Mr Leavengate as soon as you get back. And tell him where I've gone.'

She ran down the lane, climbed over a

stile, and found a narrow path in the gorse and bushes. It led her down into a shallow valley, the waist-high bushes tearing at her thin frock and stockings. She was wearing high-heeled shoes and twice within fifty yards the rough path made her stumble. Once she glanced back and saw the motionless figure of Mrs Treherne watching her, a black silhouette against the blue sky. Then the path swung away and the bushes hid the woman from sight.

Kate's mind was a turmoil as she ran on. What was the woman doing out there on the road? Was it possible she had been afraid for Sarah and had tried to warn Kate of her fear? Or was her story about Philip true, and was it Kate's own fears, only too readily aroused after the previous day's happenings, that had made her imagine the rest?

She could not be certain but knew she would never rest until Sarah was safe within her sight and protection again. She reached the bottom of the valley and started up the shallow rise opposite. The path began meandering now, skirting outcrops of rock that lay among the bushes. More than once she tried to take a more direct route but each time her insecure shoes, sinking into the heather, drove her back. She was sobbing for breath now and her eyes were half-blinded with sweat.

On reaching the crest of the shallow rise

she was forced to stop a moment to regain her breath. A glimpse of the sea again brought her both relief and a fresh sense of urgency. For on the heather-covered, rocky terrain ahead of her there was no sign of Caroline or Sarah.

She could not see far yet, however. The shallow valley she had crossed had been nothing more than an elongated basin in the cliffs and the rise had barely brought her level with the cliff surface again. Caroline and Sarah could be anywhere ahead of her on the cliff path: it was still hidden from her by a low, heather-covered ridge.

It was very quiet, the only sounds being her rapid breathing and the unperturbed song of a skylark above her. She started running again, the path leading her maddeningly around boulders, dense clumps of bushes, and shallow corries. She was nearing the top of the ridge now and a moment later caught her first sight of Penruth Cliff, the great headland on which stood the old watchtower.

The watchtower, perhaps forty feet high and built of local stone, stood at the end of the headland. It was of great age and its original purpose in some obscurity, although Kate guessed it had once served as a lighthouse to warn ships away from the rock-fanged coast. But the only time it had been occupied within living memory was during the last war when the army had erected a circular steel staircase inside it and replanked the top floor as a look-out and machine-gun post. Since then it had remained abandoned, little more than a weathered shell of tough, pitted stone.

Kate saw it as she crested the ridge, a blunt grey finger pointing up from the end of the headland. The farther-most end of the path that led to it was also visible, a thin brown scar slicing the heather at the cliff edge. She ran forward a few more yards and then saw Caroline and Sarah.

They were already on the neck of the headland, making their way in single file along the path. Sarah was leading the way, the sun bright on her bobbing chestnut hair. Caroline, in a green frock and with a satchel bag hanging from one shoulder, was immediately behind her. At this point the path was some distance from the cliff edge but as it neared the tower it veered out to within six feet of the verge.

Blind fear drove all reason from Kate's mind. She ran forward, her voice cracked and shrill. 'Sarah… Come back, darling… Your father wants you… Sarah…!'

Her voice broke off in despair. An off-sea breeze was throwing back her cries but in any case the woman and girl were too far away to hear. They were no more than fifty yards from the tower now and a ledge of rocks was driving the path nearer the cliff edge. A cluster of seagulls, perched on the rocks, rose in alarm as the couple approached. They floated round them a moment like scraps of white paper, then swooped dizzily into the abyss below where rocks lay in shelves under the lazily moving sea. Another moment and then, as Kate watched in horrified fascination, Caroline moved up alongside the unsuspecting girl.

8

It was by far the worst moment of Kate's life. Utterly helpless she could do nothing but watch as the path led Caroline and Sarah, side by side now, nearer the cliff edge where a sheer drop of four hundred feet awaited them. Every nerve in Kate's body seemed paralysed; the only thing in motion was her mind and it was in torment, flinging itself around like a frantic animal in a cage. And even it went deathly still as Caroline's arm suddenly rose behind the girl's back.

Kate turned her head sharply, closing her eyes. The silence was like distant thunder, broken only by the sibilant wash of the waves far below and the mocking song of the larks. On the brown screen of her painfully-closed eyelids red blooms seemed to swell and burst. And still she did not hear the sound she dreaded.

She forced her eyes open again. At first the cliffs swam like a drenched water-colour, so tightly had her lids been closed. Then she shook her head in astonishment. Sarah and Caroline had already passed the danger point on the path where it ran so close to the cliff edge. And now Kate saw the reason

Caroline had moved up alongside the girl – her arm was still around her waist, protecting her against the peril of a chance stumble.

If Caroline had been nearer Kate would have been forced to pour out her shame and apologise. As it was she had to steady her trembling body against a rock for a moment. She was tempted to turn back for the car but then, remembering Philip wanted Sarah, she continued down to the cliff path. By the time she reached it Caroline and Sarah had vanished into the tower.

Kate reached the tower herself five minutes later. The end of the headland was not more than fifteen yards away, a sheer drop to rocks as cruel and foam-flecked as the fangs of animals. The outer surface of the tower was the colour of the surrounding rocks, ochre-stained with lichen and weathered with age. Its door had long perished, only a stone gap remaining. After the bright sunlight the inside was cool and dark, with a faint smell of decay. Then objects began appearing from the shadows: pieces of broken timber lying on the floor, rusted tin cans, an empty ammunition box. The circular steel staircase rose from this debris and circled into the shadows above. As Kate approached it she heard the sound of voices and the hollow thud of footsteps on wooden planking. She had expected the couple above to have

162

noticed her approach but as their voices reached down to her she realised they were gazing out to sea.

'Can I look through them again, Aunt Carol?' It was Sarah's shrill excited voice.

Caroline's reply was preceded by a laugh. 'If you want to, my chick.' Then, as a swift clatter of footsteps followed: 'Don't run about like that – the planks might not be too safe.'

Kate guessed Caroline had brought binoculars with her and Sarah was now looking through them. She paused, reluctant now to draw Caroline's attention to her presence. She heard Sarah again. 'I can see the portholes this time, Aunt Carol. And people walking about on the top deck. Where do you think it's going?'

'Oh; it could be going anywhere, my chick. To America, perhaps. Or to Africa...'

Once again Kate felt shame for the enormity of her suspicions. She climbed up half a dozen of the metal steps and then called Sarah's name.

There was a pause, then the surprised scamper of Sarah's feet across the wooden planks high above. 'Kate's here, Aunt Carol. Down below somewhere...'

Kate saw Sarah now, a small shadowy figure high above at the top of the circular staircase. 'Your daddy wants you,' she called, explaining how she had met Mrs

Treherne on the road.

Sarah sounded disappointed. 'Can't he wait? It isn't anything important, is it?'

Originally Kate had felt Mrs Treherne had used Philip's name as an excuse to call Sarah back from danger. Now left to find a reason she could not think of one. 'I really don't know, darling. But I think you'd better come, just in case.'

'Oh, all right,' Sarah muttered. 'I'm sorry, Aunt Carol – Kate says I have to go back now.'

Kate waited tensely for Caroline's reaction but heard no audible comment. After warning Sarah to be careful on her way down the circular staircase she went outside. In spite of the breeze the sunlight felt warm after the darkness of the tower. A moment later Sarah followed her outside. She gave Kate a puzzled glance. 'It's funny. I saw daddy twice this morning and he never said anything about wanting me.'

'It may not be anything important,' Kate agreed. 'But as we can't be sure I think it's better you go back.'

Sarah nodded without enthusiasm. Caroline had not come down the tower yet and it was another few minutes before she appeared, grimacing fastidiously at the dust on her hands. Because of Sarah's presence her face was expressionless as she glanced at Kate. 'Hello, Miss Fielding. What's all this about Mr Leavengate wanting Sarah?'

As Kate explained it seemed to her the tiny muscles around the woman's green eyes tightened at her mention of Mrs Treherne and almost against her will her suspicions stirred again, like the silt at the bottom of a pool. She watched Caroline shrug and turn to her shoulder bag for a cigarette.

'It all sounds a bit of a mystery but I suppose it doesn't matter – we'd have had to go back for lunch soon anyway. Which will be quicker – to walk back or go with you to the car?'

'The car, I should think,' Kate told her, relieved she was not showing any open resentment.

Caroline nodded, turned to Sarah and clucked her under the chin with a slim hand. 'Come on, then, my chick, and cheer up. You break up for your holidays next week, and we can have lots of walks and picnics then.'

They walked back to the car, Sarah's chatter hiding the near silence that lay between Kate and Caroline. On reaching the house Sarah went straight to her father, who was still in his study. Kate waited in the hall outside. She noticed that Caroline, who had sauntered into the library, had left the door open behind her. A minute later Sarah came out, her oval face puzzled and resentful.

'Daddy doesn't know what we're talking about. All he did was ask Mrs Treherne where I'd gone, that was all.'

Kate suddenly realised she did not want Caroline to believe Mrs Treherne had passed on an indirect warning to her. 'Then she must have misunderstood him, dear. She did say she wasn't certain what he wanted.'

'Trust her to spoil things,' Sarah muttered sullenly. 'That's all she ever does.'

'As Aunt Carol says, you'd have had to leave for lunch a few minutes later in any case,' Kate told her. 'Better run upstairs and wash now – you're nearly black from all that dust.'

So it appeared Mrs Treherne had been trying to communicate a warning after all, Kate thought, as she went to look for John. But why – Caroline had seemed most solicitous in her care for Sarah. Kate little knew at that moment how soon the terrifying truth and the extent of Caroline's cunning was to be revealed to her.

After lunch Kate went across the fields to Wirral's cottage. John's tricycle had broken down that morning and she was going to ask Wirral to repair it. Wirral was leaving on a week's holiday that evening and she wanted to catch him before he left.

The stone cottage looked as neat as a doll's house inside its closely-cropped hedges as she entered the front garden and made her way between banks of gay summer flowers.

She was about to knock on the front door when she heard the distant rattle of crockery. Smiling she took the path round the side of the cottage, to find the back door open and Wirral at the kitchen sink. He was in his shirt sleeves, a dish plate in one hand, a drying cloth in the other. His shaggy eyebrows lifted in pleasure at seeing her.

'Hello, miss. What can I do for you?'

'John's tricycle has broken down,' she told him. 'And I am wondering if you can fix it before you leave.'

He set down the plate and dishcloth and waved her inside. 'Come in, miss, and tell me all about it.'

She followed him into his living-room, a typical countryman's with a coal fireplace, oven, table and hide three-piece suite all living together in the utmost harmony. He led her to one of the armchairs.

'Sit in that one, miss – springs are a bit softer... Will you have a cup o' tea?'

'Another time,' she told him. 'I can't stay long – I've promised to have a game of table tennis with Sarah this afternoon.'

'Spoil those kids, you do,' Wirral muttered in his husky voice, lighting one of his inevitable cigarettes. 'Run around and play with 'em more than if you were their own mother.'

She laughed at him. 'You spoil them quite a bit yourself. And anyway, it's my job to look after them.'

'Not every minute of the night and day,' he grunted. 'It's all very well – I know you're fond of 'em – but a young girl like you ought to be enjoyin' herself more – going to dances and suchlike.' He jabbed a tobacco-stained thumb in the vague direction of Whitesands. 'Let Miss Hoity-toity do a bit o' work for a change instead of lazin' around in that car of hers.'

Kate shook her head. 'You're wrong there – she works quite hard. Don't you remember my telling you – she's taken over all my secretarial work. And she's taking the children out more than she did. Only this morning she took Sarah to the old tower while I was in town. And it's quite a long walk from the house.'

Wirral gave his crooked, weatherbeaten grin. 'You mean it's a long walk for her. I thought the same thing when I saw her going there last Thursday night. Somehow you don't imagine that type walkin' further than from a cocktail bar to a taxi.'

Kate was staring at him. 'You say you saw her going to the tower? On Thursday?'

Wirral nodded. 'Aye. I was just comin' back from seein' old Jim Hardaker – you know, that old mate of mine. She was a long way off – right on the headland and the light was goin' a bit but there was no mistakin' her. No other woman in these parts does her hair up like that, that I know of. And she

168

was carryin' that satchel bag over one shoulder – I've seen her with it before.'

'Did she see you?'

'I shouldn't think so, miss. The sky was lighter over on the cliffs.'

'And you're quite sure she was going to the tower.'

'Well; she was on the headland and goin' in that direction. I didn't wait to see, o' course, but there's nothing else out there in any case.' Wirral's husky voice turned curious at all this questioning. 'Why, miss? What's been happening?'

Caroline had asked Sarah to show her the tower! And yet now it seemed she had been there herself, two days earlier... Suddenly Kate knew what she must do, if only for her peace of mind.

'Nothing,' she told Wirral, attempting a smile. 'It's just that I'm as surprised as you to hear of her doing all this walking. Now what about the tricycle? The chain's snapped – I bought a new link in St Marks this morning. Do you think you can fix it before you leave? John's lost without his old trike and I don't like bothering Mr Leavengate – he's very busy just now.'

Wirral gave his crooked, shaggy grin again. 'I reckon I can manage it, miss. Give me half an hour and I'll be over.'

Kate thanked him, chatted with him about his holidays for a few minutes, and then returned to Whitesands. After telling John about his tricycle she went into the playroom where Sarah was already waiting for her game of table tennis. 'Darling, I find I've a little errand to do, so do you mind if we leave that table tennis this afternoon? Perhaps we can have a game tomorrow, before lunch.'

Sarah took her disappointment well. 'Can I go and play with Mary and Betty then?'

Kate put an arm around her. 'Do me a favour, darling, and stay with John until I get back. I'll be as quick as I can.'

Her request awakened the girl's curiosity and forced Kate into falsehood. 'Yes, all right, Kate. But where are you going?'

'I've an appointment with a dressmaker – I'd forgotten until just now. It won't take long.' Kate went to the door before Sarah could ask any more questions. 'I'll tell John to come and play in here, shall I?'

Sarah nodded and Kate slipped out quickly. Five minutes later, wearing slacks and a stout pair of walking shoes, she made her way as unobtrusively as possible up the drive to the front gates. The morning off-sea breeze had dropped and it was a hot, sun-drenched afternoon. The path to the western cliffs and the tower lay on the other side of the road, but fearing someone might be watching her from the shining windows of Whitesands, Kate walked two hundred yards up the road before cutting across and regaining the path where it dipped behind a hill shoulder. Soon she reached the cliff path and another fifteen minutes of swift walking brought her to the headland and the tower.

It stood before her, grey, lichen-stained and somehow sinister now in spite of the hot sunshine and the singing larks. She stepped through the open entrance and instantly all was shadowy, cold and very still.

She waited for her eyes to accustom themselves to the shadows before stepping gingerly over the debris towards the circular staircase. Its metal rail felt cold to her hands as she started to climb. For some reason all the windows except those at the very top of the tower had been boarded up and as she climbed, round and round, up and up, the shadows darkened around her again. She found her heart thudding heavily, not from the effort of climbing but from some premonition. The floor of the tower, far below her now, brought her a momentary sense of giddiness and made her cling more tightly to the rail. Then the shadows began lightening again and a minute later she was climbing out into the loft at the extreme top of the tower.

It was circular in shape and perhaps twenty feet in diameter. Relics from the war were piled up against one wall; two old metal bedsteads, a deal table and two chairs, all scarred from cigarette burns, and some empty ammunition boxes. There were two windows, one facing the cliffs, a second and larger one through which the sun was at present shining, facing the sea. Through it Kate caught a dizzy glimpse of the rocks and waves far below. Both had been given wooden shutters: one was still clamped back by catches, the other had been torn off and flung away by a fierce wind. The floor was of bare wooden planks, so shrunken by the sun and weather that half-inch gaps showed between some of them. Cobwebs were everywhere, glistening silver in the sunlight.

But Kate had eyes for none of these things. They were fixed on the larger of the two windows, the one overlooking the sea. There, resting on its wide stone ledge, was a pair of small prism binoculars.

New, expensive-looking, they had an alien appearance in the decaying loft. Kate moved a few steps towards them, pausing as the floorboards creaked ominously under her feet. Then, realising Caroline must have crossed the floor herself to reach the window ledge and remembering Sarah's uninhibited scampering around the loft, she started forward again. She took one step … and without any warning the entire floor before her fell away.

It was Kate's earlier pause that saved her life. She had been standing on the central beam at that moment and it was the planks beyond it, hanging by only a thread, that gave way. If she had been walking normally her impetus would have carried her to certain death. As it was she had barely transferred her weight from the beam and so she dropped instead of being pitched forward. The beam threw her sideways as she struck it with her hip and her outflung arm struck one of the outer planks that had not fallen with the others. Clutching at it frantically she was able to prevent her body rolling into the forty-foot drop, although for the moment she was too shocked to pull herself to safety. As she hung there she heard the planks smashing into the debris below. The noise came up in hollow waves, reverberating from the stone sides of the tower. Then, as her bruised arm weakened, she realised she had only seconds left if she were to live. Somehow she managed to slide her left leg backwards, inching her body after it until the yawning pit was no longer beneath her. Then she rolled over and was safe.

She lay for minutes, lungs sobbing for air, stomach retching at the nearness of her escape. Pain stabbed her bruised hip as she forced herself to sit upright. The air was thick with dust that had risen from below: it floated in the sunbeams and she could taste it on her tongue. Still trembling she took a closer look at the gaping hole. She saw that seven planks had fallen, extending from the central beam to the beam under the window. With her head still throbbing from shock at first she could not understand it. Caroline had walked, Sarah had even run, over those very floorboards only a few hours earlier – she had heard them. Then how could they have come loose so suddenly...?

Then she began to remember ... the few minutes Caroline had taken to follow them out of the tower. Not long enough to loosen the planks, but what if they had been pre-pared some time before and had only needed a final priming to make them lethal? Would not that explain Caroline's earlier visit to the tower with her satchel bag...? And wouldn't it explain why she had warned Sarah not to run about when she herself was in the loft...?

Kate knew she could no longer afford doubts of Caroline's murderous intentions: this could be no coincidence. The trap had been prepared, an alibi established, and Sarah's mind conditioned. All that was left now was the victim to be set along the fatal path, and as Kate's eyes were drawn again to the binoculars, still lying innocently on the window ledge, she felt certain she knew how it would be done.

She found a long stick and with hands still unsteady from shock she reached gingerly over the gap to the window ledge. She tried to flick the binoculars so they fell on the planks at the side but they slid down and fell with a splinter of glass on the floor below. It did not matter: she could find them on her way down.

Her legs felt nerveless as she started down the metal staircase and she had to pause half a dozen times before reaching the floor. She soon found the binoculars, lying among the litter of splintered planks. She examined the ends of two of them but although she could see rusted holes where nails had once secured them to the beams, she could find no trace of the nails themselves.

She emerged at last into the sunlight, white-faced, her boyish crop of dark hair flecked with dust and a smear of dirt across one cheek. Her left leg and hip were bruised and her right hand skinned from contact with the rough planking. With one last glance at the tower she started painfully back to Whitesands.

To Kate's relief she gained entrance into Whitesands unobserved. She could hear a typewriter clicking behind the closed door of Philip's study as she quietly crossed the hall.

She went down the corridor to the children's playroom and listened. Her face turned anxious as she heard no sound and she opened the door and glanced inside. The room was empty but a moment later she heard children's voices from outside the house. Crossing the corridor to a window she saw with relief that Sarah and John were playing on the rear lawn. Satisfied, she hurried upstairs to her room to wash and change. She was suffering considerably from reaction now; she took two codeine tablets before going downstairs again. As she crossed the gravel apron behind the house Sarah turned and saw her. The girl's relieved expression told Kate she had been growing impatient at having to play so long with John.

'Hello,' Kate called. 'Has everything been all right while I've been away?'

Sarah's impatient tone told her nothing unusual had happened yet. 'Yes, Kate, expect that John's been silly and wouldn't play properly...'

'Have you been alone all the time? Your daddy hasn't been out. Or ... Aunt Carol?'

'No. Daddy's been working all the afternoon and I think Aunt Carol went upstairs to her room. Are you going to play table tennis with me now, Kate?'

Kate attempted a laugh and motioned to her leg. 'I've done a silly thing, darling – I've strained my leg slightly so I think we'll have to leave table tennis today. I'll get a deckchair and we'll play something out here on the lawn. Shall we get the bagatelle board? Then John can play too.'

Sarah was not enthusiastic but Kate was grimly determined to keep her in sight until Caroline attempted to spring her trap. By keeping silent about what had happened, although every nerve in her body wanted to scream it out, she was hoping a chance might present itself of catching the woman in her own net. So much depended on Caroline's own intentions. All she could do was wait and hope and try to keep her thudding heart under some control.

With the knowledge that unless coincidence had made a complete of fool of her Caroline was a cold-blooded killer, Kate found dinner that evening an unforgettable ordeal. Caroline, lovely and sophisticated in an emerald, décolleté evening gown, turning her beautiful face attentively towards Sarah, made everything, the snowy napkins, the shining cutlery, the oak-panelled walls, all part of a nightmare in which nothing was what it appeared. Kate's headache was severe now, her eyes aching, and the knowledge that behind the lovely mask that smiled at Sarah was a woman waiting to send the child to her death made her feel light-headed and giddy. The lights burned her eyes; she closed them, only to hear Philip's solicitous voice.

'You're looking very pale tonight, Kate. Don't you feel well?'

His concern was like wine, warming her

chilled and frightened body. 'I've got rather a headache,' she admitted. 'It's nothing – I'll take something for it after dinner.'

He eyed her doubtfully. 'You look to me as though you ought to be in bed. Why don't you go and I'll send Mrs Treherne up with hot milk and aspirins.'

'I'm all right, really I am,' she lied. 'It's not as bad as that.'

With dinner over Kate's tension grew. Would Caroline spring her trap that evening or would she wait? Everything pointed to that evening. It was sunlit, windless, and there were still over two hours of daylight left. And although the tower was on private land there was always the danger of a trespassing holidaymaker paying it a visit.

It happened in a way contrary to all Kate's expectations. She was out on the front lawn with Sarah, helping the girl with a huge jigsaw they had laid on a large piece of plywood. Philip had just strolled out to join them, casual now in flannels, a high-necked pullover and a yellow silk scarf. With the evening sun heightening the tan of his handsome face, his pipe jutting thoughtfully from his mouth, he was just bending forward to try a piece of the jigsaw when Caroline came through the open French windows, her high heels tap-tapping down the front terrace steps towards them.

Kate's hand went instinctively to the

pocket of her flared corduroy dress as she turned. There was a half-amused, half-puzzled expression on Caroline's face as she approached them across the closely-cut lawn. As Philip turned towards her she gave a low, self-deprecatory laugh.

'Isn't it stupid of me – I've lost my binoculars. I've turned my satchel right out but can't find them anywhere.'

Sarah's chestnut hair glinted in the sunlight as she straightened up. 'You had them this morning, Aunt Carol. When we were in the tower.'

Caroline turned to her. 'That's right, my chick. The thing is, did I leave them there or did I have them afterwards? Can you remember seeing me use them on our way home?'

Kate had expected Caroline to do anything but make the announcement as public as this. Pulses racing she waited as Sarah's face puckered in thought. 'No; the last time you had them was when we were looking at the ship. I didn't see them again.'

Caroline nodded. 'That was what I thought.' She made a moué of self-annoyance. 'Oh, well; it's too late to bother about them now. I'll go and fetch them tomorrow.' She threw a glance at Philip. 'I don't suppose there's much danger of anyone going to the tower in the meantime, is there?'

Before Philip could speak Sarah was on her feet. 'People do sometimes go there,

Aunt Carol – I've often seen them. I'll go and get them now. It won't take me long. I can go on my bicycle down the road and then cut across the cliffs – the way we came back this morning.'

Caroline's smile was all tenderness. 'You're very sweet, my chick. But won't you be just a little bit nervous going all that way alone? It's getting late for a little girl – it's better I go tomorrow.'

'Oh, bosh,' Sarah interjected. 'Why should I be nervous – I've been there dozens of times before. Haven't I, daddy?'

Philip grinned. 'I suppose you have, you little minx.'

'You see,' Sarah said triumphantly. 'I'll be back in half an hour, see if I'm not.'

Caroline turned solicitous eyes on Philip. 'Are you sure it's all right, Phil? I don't want anything to happen to her.'

Kate closed her eyes. She didn't want Sarah to go … she had them all as witnesses… If she was guilty and she must be guilty, Kate told herself fiercely – then she was as cunning as the devil himself.

Philip paused, then nodded. 'I don't see how she can come to any harm – she's got enough sense to keep away from the cliff edge.' He glanced at Sarah. 'Be careful. Walk along the path – don't run, do you hear?'

'And don't run across the floor of the loft when you go up,' Caroline warned as Sarah was about to scamper off. 'Walk slowly, the way I told you this morning.'

Kate's nails were digging deep into her clenched hands. Clever … clever … how could anyone be as fiendishly clever as this?

Philip had thrown a quick glance at Caroline. 'The floorboards aren't shaky, are they?'

Caroline wrinkled her forehead thoughtfully. 'We were both up there this morning and they seemed all right – we were there when Miss Fielding arrived.' Her casual glance at Kate was beautifully done, confirming her point without stressing it.

Philip's face cleared. 'If they took the weight of both of you they should be safe enough.' He turned back to Sarah. 'All right, off you go. Watch out for me on your way back – I'll come for a walk and meet you down the road.'

Kate never knew how she got the words out, her heart was pounding so fast. She drew her hand out of her pocket and extended it to Philip. 'There's no need for Sarah to go, Mr Leavengate. I think these are what Miss Worth left in the tower this morning.'

9

Kate was watching Caroline as she held out the binoculars to Philip. Brilliant actress though Caroline was her green eyes could not hide her shock on seeing them. They rose from the binoculars to Kate's face, and as their baffled fury licked her like a flame Kate knew at last that the worst of her suspicions were justified.

But both Philip and Sarah were staring at Kate, not Caroline. Sarah ran forward, her voice shrill with surprise. 'They're yours, Aunt Carol ... only they're broken. But how did you get them, Kate? When did you go back?'

Kate saw fear mixed with the fury in Caroline's eyes now. It gave her voice strength as she looked at Philip.

'I went back to the tower this afternoon, Mr Leavengate, and saw the binoculars lying on a window shelf. As I started towards them the floorboards in front of me gave way and fell down to the bottom of the tower. I fell but managed to catch hold of a plank and drag myself back. Later on the binoculars fell when I tried to get them – that's why they're broken.'

Beneath his tan Philip had gone very pale. 'You say this happened this afternoon?'

She nodded.

'But why haven't you told us before? I don't understand, Kate.'

Kate's accusing gaze shifted back to Caroline. 'If I hadn't gone back earlier Sarah would have been killed tonight. She'd have run across the floor and fallen straight to the bottom of the tower.' Her loathing for Caroline made her voice harsh. 'It was a deathtrap – the planks were waiting to fall.'

Before Philip, shocked at the disclosure, could speak Caroline acted. She took a step towards Kate, her voice puzzled but solicitous. 'My dear girl, what a frightful experience. Why on earth didn't you tell us before – you ought to be in bed, not out here playing with Sarah.' Then, behind her lovely sympathetic mask, her eyes burned their challenge. 'But what I can't understand is how it happened. You know yourself we were both upstairs together. And we'd been up there for over ten minutes with Sarah scampering all over the floor, hadn't we, my chick?' she asked, turning to the girl.

Sarah, whose excited face showed her only concern in the revelation was the ammunition it would provide for chatter, nodded eagerly. 'We walked all over it, Kate. And it didn't even seem shaky.'

'You see,' Caroline murmured, glancing at

Philip. 'It's very strange, isn't it?'

For a moment her audacity took Kate's breath away. Then suddenly she understood. Expecting to be accused of trying to kill Sarah, she was going to twist it so that it seemed Kate had faked the accident in order to make the accusation. And with the poison she had already skilfully injected into Philip's mind – the rueful suggestions spread over the weeks that Kate was jealous of her – such a fantastic accusation might well convince Philip she was right. For she had her alibi she had not appeared keen for Sarah to go...

No, an inner voice warned Kate; this could mean your dismissal and then all will be lost. Be as cunning as she: take her by surprise and use the accident to gain some of the ground you have lost. For there is still Billy and the school holidays are very close now...

Because of her efforts to control herself Kate's voice had an alien tone when she spoke. 'It *is* very strange, Miss Worth. Because I no sooner put my foot in the planks when they went crashing down. It's a miracle Sarah wasn't killed this morning because they can't have been safe then.'

Caroline's slim body had been tensed and ready for the accusation she believed must follow. Now confusion showed in her eyes, followed instantly by catlike fury as she realised what Kate was doing.

'But I'm telling you they were safe, Miss Fielding.'

Kate shook her head. 'They can't have been. You can't have examined them properly. Do you realise if I hadn't gone there this afternoon Sarah would have been killed when she went back tonight?' She swung round on Philip. 'Do you realise that, Mr Leavengate? It's a forty-foot drop to the bottom of the tower.'

Emotion, making her voice falter, brought Philip's supporting arm around her shoulders. His face was hidden from her by his nearness but from his voice she knew he was deeply moved.

'I don't know what to say, Kate. Or how to thank you…'

His arm, the emotion in his voice, everything united into suddenly crumbling her defences. 'I don't want thanks,' she sobbed. 'I want Sarah protected against danger. Miss Worth should never have taken such chances with a child: she ought to have made certain the floor was safe.'

He held her tighter. 'Don't worry, Kate; it won't happen again.' She felt his head lift, heard the admonition in his voice as he addressed Caroline. 'I'd never have given permission for the girl to go near the place if I'd guessed anything like this might happen.'

Holding back her sobs, Kate listened to Caroline. 'But Phil, I tell you the floor was perfectly safe when we were there. Is Miss Fielding certain she didn't do something to make it collapse?'

Here it was – the line she would have taken had Kate accused her. But Kate felt confident of its failure now. She raised her head. 'I've told you – I no sooner touched the boards with my foot when they collapsed. There weren't even any nails in them when I examined them later. Go and see for yourself if you don't believe me.'

Caroline shrugged. 'Then they must have been tampered with after we left this morning. There's no other explanation.'

Philip made an exclamation of impatience. 'That's absurd, Carol. Why should anyone do a thing like that?'

For a moment Kate wondered breathlessly if she was going to overplay her hand. But she was far too clever. Her voice suddenly dropped, became gently remonstrative. 'Please remember one thing, Phil. I didn't want Sarah to go tonight. She offered and you agreed. If I'd had my way I'd have gone myself in the morning.'

Kate moved away from Philip as his voice became more impatient. 'That's quite true, but I don't see the connection. What I'm saying – and I think Kate's saying it too – is that the loft must have been dangerous this morning and you can't have examined it properly before taking Sarah up there. I won't mince words, Carol – when a child has just missed death I don't think I should. In the future I'd like you to be much more careful where you take the children.'

In the brief silence that followed Kate could imagine the fury raging inside the woman as she forced a look of contrition on her face. Her slim shoulders lifted, dropped regretfully, and she turned away. As Sarah's anxious gaze followed her, she dropped one of her hands on the girl's chestnut hair. 'Your daddy doesn't think I've taken good enough care of you today, my chick, and perhaps he's right.' She suddenly bent down and kissed the girl's cheek, an act with all the hallmarks of spontaneous emotion. 'Anyway, thanks to Miss Fielding, you're safe, darling, and that's all that really matters.' She straightened and threw a contrite glance back at Philip. 'I'm very sorry, Phil, and can only thank God things have worked out this way. I'll see you later.'

Philip's nod was curt and he made no effort to call her back as she went up the front terrace and into the house, every movement of her slim body expressing self-reproach. Kate was inwardly praying Sarah would not follow her but after hesitating a moment the girl stayed with them. Her face was troubled now as she looked up at her father.

'It wasn't her fault, daddy. It wasn't, honestly.'

Philip did not reply, motioning down at the jigsaw instead. 'You clear this up and take it inside. I don't think any of us feel like playing tonight.' He turned to Kate. 'Do you feel like telling me more about it? Or would you rather go in and rest now?'

Kate shook her head, told him what happened from the moment she entered the loft to her examining the fallen planks at the bottom of the tower. When she finished his expression was more perplexed than ever.

'None of this explains why you went back this afternoon. That seems the oddest thing of all.'

As she stood there with him, the setting sun making slim giants of their shadows on the lawn, she felt eyes watching them. Caroline would be standing behind one of Whitesands' shining windows, watching to see if she told him of her suspicions. With Philip's blue-grey eyes warmer than Kate had ever known them her temptation was fierce but she knew it could do nothing but harm. Carelessness on Caroline's part he had accepted. But it was in a different world from attempted child murder.

'I really don't know,' she lied. 'I just felt like a walk and my legs took me there. Perhaps it was because I'd heard Sarah talking to Caroline about the view from up there and subconsciously I wanted to see it myself...'

'If it was chance it's the nearest thing to

Providence I've ever known,' he said quietly. 'I'm never going to be able to repay this, Kate.'

Her eyes followed Sarah, who was taking the jigsaw up the terrace to the open French windows of the library. A sudden shiver ran through her. 'Just always see Sarah is safe. That's all.'

He put a hand on her arm, drew it affectionately to him. 'Come inside and have a drink. That's what you should have had hours ago. And it's getting chilly out here.'

She was only too glad to follow Sarah although the girl had vanished by the time they entered the library. Inside it was all rich sunlight and velvet shadows. He checked her, took hold of her shoulders, and turned her gently towards him.

'You still haven't explained why you didn't tell us about this as soon as you got back.'

She had been expecting the question. 'I suppose it was because I felt a bit of a fool about the whole thing.'

'Did you know those binoculars belonged to Caroline when you first saw them on the window ledge?'

She hesitated. Sarah had left the library door ajar; she wondered if Caroline were listening. 'Not really,' she lied.

'And yet, although they were broken, you brought them back and even had them outside in your pocket. Why was that, Kate?'

She knew she could provide no really satisfactory answers. 'I don't really know why I had them. I was going to tell you about the collapse of the floor, of course, but there just hadn't seemed an opportunity before...'

'There was the whole of dinner time,' he reminded her.

She tried to smile. 'As I say, I think I felt rather stupid and clumsy at nearly breaking my neck. I'm sure that was my reason.'

She knew she had not convinced him. There was a look of perplexity in his blue-grey eyes that she was to notice often in the five short days left before the final crisis. But now, at this reminder of her near death, his hands which were still resting on her shoulders gripped tighter and pulled her towards him. 'Thank God it didn't happen, Kate. It doesn't bear thinking of...'

Something as gentle as a butterfly's wing brushed her hair. Then, before she had time to move to speak, he released her and turned away.

'Let's go into the sitting-room and have that drink,' he said almost curtly, moving towards the door. She stood motionless for a moment, one hand reaching up and touching her hair. A strange singing had begun inside her – then she shook her head impatiently. It was only reaction on his part: it had no significance. But her face was very pale as she followed him out into the hall.

Kate lay awake for hours that night. Although commonsense told her that any new attempt Caroline might make on Sarah's life would have to be elaborately contrived to keep her free of suspicion and would therefore be most unlikely to occur inside the house, she nevertheless started at every creak in the corridor and visited Sarah's room half a dozen times before midnight. At last, seeing the key in the girl's bedroom door, she locked the door on the outside, left a small light burning in the corridor and left her own bedroom door open.

Yet still she could not sleep. Her leg and hip ached from her fall and a devil doubt kept asking her if she were right in not telling Philip of her suspicions. For then he would at least have been warned, and the awful responsibility of guarding Sarah would not have been hers alone...

Her instincts fought the doubt. To Philip the accusation would be fantastic and if it resulted in her dismissal from Whitesands – and Caroline would then have excellent cause to demand it – Sarah would be left entirely at her mercy. It was true that if anything subsequently happened to Sarah, Philip would be reminded of Kate's suspicions, but what use would it be then? And Caroline was so clever the odds would still be in favour of her emerging unscathed.

When Kate's mind finally allowed her to

sleep she was flung into the worst nightmare of her life. She was back again in the tower, this time an enormous edifice whose circular staircase led her upwards through a dark void, at kind of purgatory from which voices moaned eerily at her. She would have gone back in her terror but for some secret knowledge that in the darkness above her Sarah was in peril.

An unnatural cold sank into her as she climbed. The invisible voices grew more urgent. 'Go back,' they moaned. 'Go back before it is too late…' But then she believed she heard Sarah's voice and her feet flew up the staircase, round and round, up and up, while the voices seemed to coalesce into a lament of despair.

And then she saw the reason. Two green eyes, like coals of phosphorus, had risen from the darkness and were now floating alongside the staircase. Sobbing with fear she ran on while the eyes followed her effortlessly.

Then, quite suddenly, she was in the loft – a frightening place of icy moonlight and jet-black shadows. Sarah was there, wide-eyed, wearing a pretty flounced dress, her oval face unbearably innocent and child-like. Arms outstretched Kate ran towards her. 'Sarah, darling, come away at once. It's dangerous here. Sarah, do you hear me…?'

The girl did not turn her head. Her fascinated eyes were staring across the loft. Kate followed them and terror stabbed her like a dagger of ice.

Caroline was standing before the window, motionless in an ice-cold moonbeam. She had the terrible loveliness of a lamia, lips as red as freshly-spilled blood, eyes as green as the Arctic sea. The rest of her, slender body, hair now hanging down almost to her waist, her face: all had the cold whiteness of the moonlight. As Kate watched her red lips smiled invitingly. She lifted a hand and beckoned Sarah to approach her.

Voices rose from below, moaning in torment. And then Kate saw the floor before the woman was a blacker pool of darkness than the rest. Frantic now she clutched at Sarah but as her hands seemed to slip through the girl she realised with fresh horror that her own body had no substance, that Sarah could neither see nor feel her.

The lamia at the window beckoned again and Sarah stepped forward like a sleep walker. Kate screamed and the woman turned towards her, smiling a devil's smile with her red, red lips...

Kate awoke with a great start, her sweat-drenched pyjamas icy against her body. The first grey light of morning was seeping through the window. Before her the light in the corridor shone through her open bedroom door, and for a moment it seemed a slender figure was standing there, gazing at her as Caroline had gazed at Sarah. Whether it was a last shredding mist from her nightmare or a real figure she had no way of telling, for as her body jerked upright it vanished and when she reached the door the corridor was empty.

Shivering with cold she fetched the key, unlocked Sarah's room, and then lay sleepless, waiting for the day to come.

As it was Sunday Kate was able to keep an eye on Sarah without undue difficulty and it proved an uneventful day. At the same time she longed for an ally with whom to share her fears and bitterly regretted that Wirral should be away on holiday at the very time her suspicions were confirmed. She thought of Dereck Redfearn, but she had not seen him for weeks and also she remembered his love of gossip. If Philip discovered her suspicions second-hand from Dereck it would be worse than making a direct accusation. In thinking of him and Wirral, however, she remembered Mrs Treherne. Her warning, veiled though it had been, had proved wellfounded – would she not do the same again if her suspicions were aroused? Kate felt an approach to her must be made, particularly as Caroline's infinite resourcefulness had made her think of food poisoning in connection with Sarah.

She chose the late afternoon, when she was fetching John's dinner from the kitchen, to talk to the housekeeper. Sarah was out in the back garden with her father at the time: Kate could hear their voices through one of the open windows of the corridor. The kitchen door was open: she could see Mrs Treherne's broad back as she stood over a pan on the stove. Kate went inside and closed the door behind her.

'I've come for John's dinner, Mrs Treherne. He said you told him it was ready.'

Without turning her head the dark-skinned, stocky woman motioned to a tray on a nearby table. 'It's over there. I'm just boilin' the milk – it won't be a moment.'

Kate went over to the tray, then said quietly, 'Did you hear what happened yesterday afternoon, Mrs Treherne? In the tower?'

The housekeeper stiffened, then turned sharply, her small black eyes on Kate's face. 'Happened, miss? What did happen?'

Quietly Kate told her about her second visit to the tower and how the floor had collapsed as she went forward to pick up the binoculars. 'Late in the evening Miss Worth discovered they were missing and Sarah volunteered to fetch them,' she went on. 'If I hadn't gone there earlier she'd certainly have been killed.'

One of the housekeeper's blunt hands had clutched her apron, the knuckles white against the brown skin. Her tongue wet her lips.

'I thought you mightn't have heard,' Kate said. 'And I felt you ought to know.'

The small frightened eyes became instantly wary. 'What d'you mean? Why ought I to know?'

Kate took a deep breath. 'Mrs Treherne, you were afraid something was going to happen to Sarah yesterday morning – you all but said so out there on the road. If you know anything it's your duty to come with me to Mr Leavengate at once. You must – you can't leave a child in danger.'

The housekeeper threw a quick glance at the closed door. Again her tongue wet her lips as she turned back to Kate. 'I don't know what you're talkin' about,' she muttered hoarsely. 'I went out because I thought Mr Leavengate wanted her – that was all.'

'That's not true. You were frightened. You're frightened now. What is it, Mrs Treherne? Tell me before it's too late.'

Again the woman glanced at the door. At that moment the milk boiled over with a loud hiss, startling them both. While Mrs Treherne attended to it Kate, her pulses racing, went to the door and pulled it open. The corridor was empty. She closed the door and turned back. 'Miss Worth isn't there, so you can tell me the truth. I don't know what you've done but if you can help me I'll do all I can for you. I promise that.'

For a moment the woman's swarthy face blurred as if conflicting emotions were at war behind it. Then it set like grey cement. 'I don't know what you're talkin' about – comin' in here and sayin' such things. I've told you all I know and that's nothing. Take your tray and let me get on with my work.'

Kate realised the woman was in too deep. 'All right, Mrs Treherne, but remember this. I know what's going on and if anything should happen to that child I'll make very sure that everyone involved gets their full deserts. You'll be in serious trouble in law, you know, if it comes out that you knew what was going to happen and made no effort to prevent it. You might be found guilty of being an accomplice.'

The silence was dour, flint-like. But as Kate turned for the door the woman's sullen voice checked her. 'I don't know what you're talkin' about, miss, and I'll say it again. But if you're meaning you're afraid of the girl havin' an accident here in the house, maybe with food or some such thing, then you don't have to worry. I'm careful with that, and I keep my eyes and ears open as I go around too.'

It was as much as Kate had hoped for in the beginning and in her loneliness she felt almost warm to the woman as she faced her again. 'I'm glad to hear that, Mrs Treherne.

For your sake as much as anybody's, it's important nothing happens to Sarah. Remember, if you change your mind and tell me all you know, I'll do my very best to help you.'

The housekeeper, her face grey beneath its grimness, made no further comment and Kate took the tray from the kitchen.

Monday, a day Kate had been dreading, came all too soon. At dinner the previous night Caroline had been all graciousness and contrition, but once or twice Kate had caught her eyes resting on her and had shivered at the cold fury she had known was raging behind them. Now, alone in the house with her and Mrs Treherne, she dared not think what the day might bring. Had it been fine she would have tried to escape by taking John for a picnic but a chilly wind had sprung up during the night and by ten o'clock squalls of rain were beating the front windows of Whitesands.

A malevolent atmosphere hung over the house which the grey day outside did nothing to lighten. Kate felt it wherever she went, malignant and growing more dangerous as time ran out. Instinct told her the explosion must come soon now, although how and when she could not guess.

So far she had not seen Caroline that morning. The woman had not come down for breakfast, nor was she in the library or sitting-room now. But Kate knew she could be behind any of the numerous closed doors that lined Whitesands' corridors and every time she had to leave the playroom, which she had established as a kind of citadel for John and herself, she had to summon up all her courage. Since Saturday she had not met Caroline alone and she was dreading the ordeal.

But it was not until nearly midday that the meeting occurred. The rain had stopped and John wanted to go out and play in the garden. Kate sent him to fetch a coat from his room but he was unable to find it. Forced to go herself she almost took John with her, feeling his presence might prevent an incident, but in the end shame won and she went alone.

Her heart was hammering painfully when she reached the upstairs landing. But Caroline's room door was closed and the corridor empty and quiet. With bated breath Kate started down it, walking as quietly as possible. She reached John's room without interruption, found his coat and was half-way back to the landing when she heard sudden quick footsteps. Face paling she hurried forward but Caroline was too quick, reaching the top of the staircase before her.

She was wearing a high-necked sweater, russet-coloured slacks and mules. Her ash-blonde hair was loose, tumbling in waves down her shoulders. As she swung round Kate had a feeling of recognition. It was the lamia of her nightmare again, with the pale face, blood-red lips and terrible eyes. Only now she was not smiling her evil, seductive smile. Her face was thinned, her lips drawn back as though by tiny wires.

'I've been waiting to see you alone – waiting since Saturday. You're to leave Whitesands, do you hear? I don't care what excuse you give Mr Leavengate but you're to go this week. Do you understand?'

Kate's throat felt closed, painful. 'Must I? Why?'

The hate in the green eyes was frightening. 'You know why. You knew that floor was safe but you had to make out I'd been careless. I'm having no more of your lies and insinuations. Go back to London – meddle in some office if you must meddle, but get out of this house.'

Defiance began flowing back into Kate through a thousand tiny channels. 'Was I meddling, then, when I saved Sarah's life?'

Caroline's malignancy became almost palpable. Throwing aside all pretence her low voice came to Kate like a soft but ice-laden wind. 'If I were you I shouldn't worry too much about Sarah. Accidents can happen to other people too – people who meddle in things that aren't their affair. Pack your things and go, Miss Fielding. I shan't give you another warning.'

She was gone a second later but her threat hung like rime in the hushed corridor.

10

Tuesday followed, an endless day but one without any incident. Wednesday came and Kate felt she must soon crack under the strain. The days were long enough but the nights seemed endless. She would lie awake, starting at the faintest sound, tension like a steel wire around her temples and tightening every time the clocks chimed away another hour. What would Caroline's next step be? Time was running out fast – only Thursday remained before the school holidays. Would she strike before then or would she wait in the hope that Billy would not return to St Marks? He might not – the thought made Kate feel physically sick – his treatment at Whitesands might easily have turned him against another holiday in Cornwall. If that happened Caroline would have won – it was certain she would see Kate was forced to leave Whitesands before another school holiday came round. Or else see she was involved in an accident ... Kate knew she had meant her threat.

She dared not think of failure. Her plan was to take Sarah into St Marks early on Friday morning, spend the whole day in the park looking for Billy if need be, and not return home until the late evening. Philip worked late on Thursdays and Fridays – they might even arrange to come back with him. While Kate felt it unlikely Billy would arrive so early in the holidays it would at least keep them both out of Caroline's reach for the day. The weekend was uncertain – they would go into St Marks if Kate could think of some excuse to give Philip. But the following week they would go every day – Kate had already discussed this in private with Sarah and with Billy as the prize the girl was only too eager. Beyond that date, if Billy had not appeared, Kate's mind would not reach. As she felt at the moment a week was an eternity.

When Thursday arrived without incident she felt both hope and increased tension. Was it possible Caroline had decided to wait and see first if Billy returned to Cornwall? Certainly it seemed she could do little now before Friday – to celebrate the commencement of the summer holidays Dr Dundas was taking his two daughters and Sarah to tea and a cinema show that evening, Sarah meeting them after school. So, until the doctor brought the girl back to Whitesands in the region of nine-thirty, she was safe from Caroline.

There was nothing, therefore, that day to warn Kate how near the crisis was except the weather. It began with an excessively bright morning that began hazing over until by lunch-time a brassy cloud covered the whole sky. It trapped the heat and increased the humidity until Kate felt her racked nerves would snap. To escape from Whitesands she packed food and took John out on the cliffs in the afternoon. Because of the oppressive cloud and the glassy sea she dared not go far but the storm held off and she stayed out until the child's bedtime. After he was washed and safely tucked into bed she fetched a book and returned to his room. Even asleep he was company for her and from his window she commanded a view of the cliff road. It was her intention to run downstairs the moment she saw the doctor's car and escort Sarah into the house.

The heat made John restless. About eight o'clock he awoke and Kate had to soothe him to sleep again. She pushed the window wider in an effort to get more air into the room. There was not a vestige of wind, the curtains hung limp and motionless. As she listened she could hear the sullen murmur of the sea. A bird fluttered restlessly in the ivy outside the window, then the silence returned, more oppressive than before.

As Kate sat at the window a woman walked out on the lawn below. Her pulse began racing as she recognised the slim figure of Caroline; until that moment she had not been certain whether the woman was in the house or not. She appeared to be taking a breath of air but a restlessness about her made Kate think of a cat, prowling about in an effort to reach a prey that had so far escaped it. Twice she threw a glance up at the east wing and each time Kate drew quickly back, breath held in case she was seen. When the woman finally vanished back into the house she did not know whether to feel relief or increased fear.

From somewhere below a clock chimed, followed by the sycophantic echo of the old grandfather clock on the upstairs landing. Nine o'clock. Sarah would be home soon. The cloud above was like a huge animal now, pressing its hot furry body on the ground below. It darkened the twilight and brought shadows into the bedroom. Kate could no longer read; she put aside her book and listened. The first distant rumble of thunder sounded, the murmur of the sea following like an echo.

Nine-fifteen, and Kate's nerves were taut wires. The slowness of the storm's approach was almost sadistic, although it could now be heard grumbling over the sea like a savage animal. The heat was stifling; John kept tossing about and muttering in his sleep. Suddenly he let out a distressed cry and sat bolt upright. His wide frightened eyes did not recognise Kate immediately as she hurried over to him. She put an arm around his shoulders. His body was hot and his pyjamas soaked in sweat.

'It's nothing, darling,' she soothed. 'Only a dream. Close your eyes and go to sleep again.'

His voice was drowsy and confused. 'I'm thirsty. I want a drink...'

There was a glass of water at his bedside; Kate held it to his lips. 'There you are, darling. Now put your head down on your pillow... That's right.'

He had been only half-conscious and was asleep almost immediately. As Kate straightened she heard the slam of a car door: in comforting John she had missed hearing the approach of Dr Dundas's smooth-running car. Heart thudding she ran to the window. In the gloom she could see the car outside the gates and heard Sarah's voice. 'Thanks ever so much, Dr Dundas – it was super. See you tomorrow...'

The car turned to drive away. Sarah ran through the gates and up the drive. Before Kate could move the girl's sharp eyes pierced the gloom and saw her. She ran immediately off the drive and on to the terrace below. Kate could see the excitement on her face as she stared up.

'Kate; I've got such marvellous new...' Her voice was shrill, stabbing holes in the thick silence. 'Billy's here – already. I saw him at lunch-time. Isn't it wonderful...?'

Now, Kate thought, all hell will break loose...
She wanted to cry out to the girl to keep quiet but for the moment her throat was gripped as if in a vice. She gazed in horror at the child's innocent, excited face below.

'He's staying a whole month this time, Kate. And I've got this address in St Marks. Isn't it just super...?'

Kate could not recognise her voice. 'Darling, come upstairs at once. Come in the side door and I'll meet you in the hall.'

Sarah looked puzzled now. 'What's the matter, Kate? You're looking ever so queer.'

Kate, in agony, tried to keep her words from being overheard. 'Don't ask questions now, darling. Hurry, please. It's very important.'

The girl threw her a last perplexed glance and then turned for the drive. Kate wanted to scream at her to hurry but knew Caroline would be listening. Turning, she ran down the corridor. The shadows were dense, the silence made more intense by the slow, asthmatical tick of the grandfather clock. Halfway down the stairs she paused. There were no lights in the hall: it was shadowy and very sinister. Then she heard the slam of an outer door and quick, buoyant footsteps. She ran down the rest of the stairs, reaching the hall as Sarah appeared. She caught hold of the girl's arm. 'Come upstairs with me, darling. Quickly.'

She began to look frightened. 'What's the matter, Kate? What's happened?'

Kate could see nobody in the hall but she knew menacing ears were listening. Somehow she had to gain a few more precious minutes... 'Nothing's happened, darling – what makes you think that? I've just got a nice surprise upstairs to show you, that's all.'

She half-dragged the girl upstairs. She ran into Sarah's room, grabbed a mackintosh and pushed the girl's arms into it. 'Now, listen, darling. There's no time for questions – you must do exactly as I say. We're going to your father and it's vital that neither your Aunt Carol nor Mrs Treherne finds out. So go as quietly as you can and don't speak unless I speak to you first. Do you understand?'

Sarah's eyes were huge in the gloom. She swallowed nervously and nodded. Kate held her tightly for a moment and kissed her pale cheeks. 'That's a brave girl... Just try to pretend it's a game we're playing – that we're trying to get out of the house without anyone else knowing.'

Distant lightning gleamed through the open door of John's room, lighting up the corridor for a split second before allowing the shadows to return more dense than ever. Thunder growled a few seconds later. The storm was closing in; the crisis was at flashpoint. Kate ran and closed John's door. She hated leaving the child but knew he was not the one in danger.

She hurried Sarah down a side corridor that led to the west wing of Whitesands, expecting Carol to appear at any moment either behind them or in one of the closed doors that lined the corridor. Lightning flashed again, adding a nightmare touch to their flight. In the silence that followed the thunder Kate heard Sarah's frightened breathing. She pressed the girl's hand tightly. 'Be a brave girl,' she whispered. 'You'll soon be safe with your daddy.'

'But why aren't I safe here, Kate? What are we running away from?'

Kate hushed her. 'I can't tell you now. Later, darling – when we've got away.'

They turned into the west wing corridor. On their left yawned a wide staircase. Ignoring it Kate hurried on. Beyond it was a narrower staircase leading to a one-time tradesmen's entrance at the rear of the house. Once it had provided an access for maids to reach their quarters but today it was seldom used.

Kate led the way down it. The steps were uncarpeted and she motioned Sarah to tread lightly. As they turned a sharp corner thunder rolled again, muffled now by the mass of the house above them. It was very dark on the stairs and Kate had to feel her way. She tried to imagine what Caroline was doing. She must have heard Sarah talking about Billy. Would she have an emergency plan that she was already putting into action? Or was she improvising one now with that frightening, razor-sharp brain of hers?

Another sharp corner and they reached the foot of the stairs. They were in a lumber room now, a place filled with old tools and derelict pieces of furniture. The air was hot and fusty. Bare water pipes festooned the walls; a large water cistern stood in a shadowy recess. Water, gurgling uneasily along one of the pipes, made Kate turn sharply. In the gloom Sarah's face was very white.

'Why are we running away, Kate? Please tell me.'

'Later, darling. Please don't talk now.'

The lock of the door was badly rusted and at first Kate could not turn the key. Then it gave with a grating sound. The hinges groaned loudly as she drew the door carefully open. A hot wind, heavy with the scent of hyacinths, blew in, then the air was still again.

Pulses throbbing, Kate edged out. It was uncannily quiet. The lawns and flowerbeds of the back garden were on her left, shadowy in the deepening gloom. The rear of the house was in darkness except for a diffused gleam of light in one of the upstairs windows. Finger on her lips Kate motioned Sarah to follow her.

There was a gravel path alongside of the

house, running the full length of the back gardens. It was shielded from the lawns and the house by a row of bushes and shrubs and Kate led Sarah along it, heading for the fields beyond. Thirty seconds later they reached the huge bank of rhododendrons that stood at the end of the gardens. Kate paused there a moment and glanced back. The house was still silent, without movement. Then, as another flash of lightning lit up Sarah's white face, Kate drew the girl into the bushes and hurried her on.

They climbed a stile over a stone wall and were in the first of the fields beyond Whitesands. A few large spots of rain fell, then stopped. It was almost dark now. Feeling they would be less silhouetted against the sky Kate made Sarah walk alongside one of the stone walls. Something dark loomed up ahead of them, shied away. Kate's heart thudded until she realised it was only a cow. They came across four more of the animals a few seconds later, huddled together as they waited for the storm to break.

They climbed over another stile and hurried on. The house behind them still showed no signs of activity and Kate's hopes began to rise. If they could once reach the main trunk road to St Marks she felt their chances of escape were good. Even at this time of night there was always some traffic on it, as well as a bus service to St Marks. Her concern was the feeder road that lay ahead. It carried few cars at night and it was two and a half miles to the trunk road.

As if to illustrate her thoughts a car's headlights rose up from behind a hill to the east, probed the dense sky and then fell away. That was the road they must reach, as quickly as possible. She caught Sarah's arm again. 'Hurry, darling. Start running again. You'll understand why later on.'

They ran across the field to the next stile. Sweat was running into Kate's eyes and soaking through her thin dress. The humidity was stifling, making it difficult to force air into her gasping lungs. If only the rain would come it would be easier to think what the devil-eyed woman in Whitesands might be planning...

They jumped down from the stile into the third field. A group of startled cows shied away, hoofs thudding in the silence. A car passed along the road ahead, its headlights searching out the mossy stone walls. How long would it be before another came, Kate thought, watching its red tail-light vanish over a distant rise.

Lightning, much closer now, brought a reeling glimpse of fields, walls, and the distant moors. The thunder and the darkness that followed it made Sarah fumble for Kate's hand.

One last field and they reached the road.

Kate found a gate and pulled it open. A smell of thistles rose in the hot sullen air. White-sands was now a dark, almost invisible silhouette on the cliffs. But as Kate pulled the gate closed a sudden light appeared in one of the upstairs windows. As she froze and watched another appeared and yet another...

In her mind she was suddenly a terrified spectator back in the house, hiding as Caroline, discovering they were missing, combed the house from room to room. She would be like a furious panther, thin-faced and murderous. More lights appeared as the tempo of the search quickened. Sarah pressed close to Kate.

'Are they looking for us, Kate?'

'Yes, darling. They've discovered we're not in our rooms.'

The girl was very close to tears. 'But why does it matter, Kate? Aunt Carol's always been so nice to me. Why are we running away?'

'There's no time to tell you now, darling. You'll understand everything when we're safe with your daddy. Now come along – we've a long way to go yet.'

Half-running, half-walking, they started down the road. Complete darkness had fallen now. The sullen air was like stagnant water, resisting their progress. Kate bit back a cry of fear as something brushed her hair. It was a bat, flitting about near the ground in the heat and humidity. The road took them up a long, shallow rise. Kate was driving Sarah faster now and the girl was sobbing for breath. Lightning ripped the black sky apart, thunder was like an enormous calico sheet being torn, but still the rain did not come. In the darkness that followed Sarah stumbled over the grass verge. Kate picked her up. 'Hurry, darling. We must reach the main road as quickly as possible.'

Halfway up the shallow rise Kate glanced back. Whitesands was ablaze with lights now as if celebrating some great occasion. Lightning flashed over the moors: the storm seemed to be circling about like a great predatory bird before launching its fury earthward. When silence returned Kate listened but still could not hear the sound she feared. Heartened, she urged Sarah on. 'We'll soon be there, darling. Try to keep going.'

For a few minutes Whitesands disappeared from view as the road dipped over the rise. Kate herself was tiring now: her lungs were burning and her legs aching. Sarah was sobbing with weariness and fear, and Kate knew she would have to give her a short rest. As they reached the bottom of the rise, with Whitesands once again in view, she caught hold of the girl's hand.

'Stop a moment, darling,' she panted. 'Get your breath back before we go on.'

Exhausted herself it was a relief to rest on

the grass verge, her arms around the panting, trembling girl. But as her breath returned so did her anxiety. The main road must still be well over a mile away; every second was precious…

Yet she dared not drive Sarah too hard. 'How do you feel now, darling?' she asked anxiously. 'We mustn't be too long.'

The girl was openly sobbing now. 'I've got a stitch in my side … it hurts me…'

'I'm so sorry, darling. But I have to get us both away from Aunt Carol. You see, she isn't the nice person you and your daddy have always thought; I couldn't let you stay with her any longer.'

Sarah's eyes were shining pools of fear in the darkness. 'But why haven't you told me before? Why have we to run away tonight?'

Kate pressed her cheek to the girl's sweating, tear-soaked face. 'You'll understand everything once we reach your father. And that won't take long if you're a brave girl – once we reach the main road we'll soon be in town.'

Her assurances, such as they were, seemed to calm the girl. Kate drew back, smiled at her. 'Well; are you ready to start off again?'

Sniffing back her tears Sarah nodded doubtfully. 'I think so – if we don't run too much. I've still got the stitch in my side.'

Kate was about to reply when a hot movement of air brought the sound she had been dreading – the distant but unmistakable whine of a sports car engine being revved up. The darkness around them became full of terror again and she seized Sarah's arm.

'Never mind your side. Come on – run as fast as you can...'

She urged the girl on into the darkness. Her intention was to get as near as possible to the trunk road before taking to the fields, for no matter how furiously Caroline drove she still had to go all the way around by the hamlet. It was the greatest mistake of her life, but at that moment her mind was too panic-stricken to remember what lay ahead.

As if the storm were in league with Caroline the lightning ceased for a moment, giving her no chance to see where the road was leading them. They stumbled on for two agonised minutes, three minutes... Sarah was sobbing again and clutching her side. As Kate tried to support her she heard the hum of a fast approaching engine.

So soon – she had not believed it possible. But already a luminous mist was growing on the crest of the rise behind them. Kate turned back, searching desperately for a gap in the walls. But the silver mist appeared to have dazzled her; the walls now seemed to tower blackly into the sky. She felt for the grass verge with her foot and to her horror felt an almost vertical bank. Then she remembered and could have cried aloud at her mistake. They had run into the long cutting topped by impenetrable bushes and trees that lay at the foot of the hill overlooking St Marks.

Now, mocking them, the lightning returned, revealing the high, unscalable banks on either side of the road. As darkness swooped back Kate threw a glance over her shoulder. The luminous mist was fast growing brighter; unless they could find a gap somewhere they were trapped. She pushed Sarah forward.

'Keep running, darling... Try to find somewhere to hide.'

The silver mist began to illuminate the road. Kate saw something dark on the bank thirty yards ahead of them. It was indistinct: it might only be a shadow but there was nothing else and Kate urged Sarah towards it. Three seconds ... four seconds ... and then the car headlights leapt over the rise and dropped exultantly on them.

Kate had never felt so exposed in her life. The high unscalable banks on either side of the narrow road, the long fingers of shuddering light that held them like flies on a pin. Like a scream of triumph the note of the engine rose to an even higher pitch, and as quick as a photoflash a vision of Caroline flashed through Kate's tormented mind. She would be crouched behind the wheel, lovely face thin with hate, green eyes exultant. And in the same split second Kate knew what was coming – the razor-sharp brain would not fail to clutch what fate was offering her. Two road casualties … an unknown hit-and-run driver … who would ever suspect her, and if they did Mrs Treherne could always be frightened into providing an alibi…

In the same instant of revelation Kate saw the nature of the shadow on the bank. It was part of the roots of a tree, clawing down the bankside like a gnarled hand to within three feet of the road. It offered little protection for them both, being raised little more than eighteen inches from the soil, but it might provide a foothold for Sarah…

Only seconds were left, the scream of racing metal and tyres was growing louder at every moment. Frantically Kate pushed the hysterical girl up the bank. 'Catch hold of it, darling. Pull yourself up. Hurry, for God's sake…'

The lights were blinding now, like the spotlights on a stage. They revealed Sarah's chalk-white face and terrified eyes. She was lying over the mossy roots, her legs straddling them. If she had lain on one side there might have been a chance for Kate to cling to the other, but as it was she almost pulled the girl down in an attempt to climb up after her.

If there had been time to make Sarah understand she might have been able to find a foothold herself. But there was no time … the car was only seconds away. She would have to try to jump up the bank at the exact moment the car reached her… Of all the thoughts that flashed in fantastic succession through her mind in those last few seconds one, the most bitter, was that if she jumped too late or rolled back under the car all her efforts to save Sarah's life would have been in vain. As she waited, hypnotised by the noise and sight of the car screaming straight at her, a thick bead curtain seemed to drop between her and the brilliant headlights. The storm had broken at last, the rain bounding waist-high from the road. It was her last conscious impression before the enormous, crushing headlights filled her whole vision.

11

It was a moment Kate was to remember all her life and yet, as such moments of danger are, it was composed of fragmentary impressions rather than a continuity of detail. The terrifying scream of the car engine, the wild hiss of its tyres, its two brilliant headlights behind which she could just discern a black mass of metal hurling itself at her, and the sudden downpour of rain that drenched her sweating body: these were the major impressions in the last two seconds before she leapt for the bank. It was after her leap that her impressions broke into smaller fragments – Sarah's terrified scream ... her own hands clawing frantically at the grassy bank in a vain effort to prevent herself toppling back on the road ... a blow of air like a huge fist in her side. Then a tremendous thud that seemed to make the bank reel ... an agonised squeal of brakes and tyres ... and a massive rending of metal and splintering glass that seemed to continue for minutes while she lay dazed and drenched on the road, unable to believe she was still alive.

It was Sarah's terrified sobbing that pulled her together. In the darkness that had swooped back the frantic girl was tugging at her. 'Kate … are you hurt? Say something to me, Kate… Please say something…'

Lying there in the torrential rain, her dress soaked and shoes full of water, Kate could just make out Sarah's face, a shapeless white blur in the darkness. Somehow she managed to climb to her feet. 'I'm all right, darling. What about you? Are you hurt at all?'

The enormous relief in the girl's voice almost made Kate break down. 'Oh, Kate; I thought you were dead. I'm so frightened, Kate … I want to go home…'

Kate was acutely conscious of the smell of hot oil as she tried to comfort the hysterical girl. As lightning flashed again she saw the car. With all its lights extinguished it lay at the foot of the bank about forty yards away, unrecognisable as the sleek and lovely thing it had been a few minutes earlier. Another object impressed itself on the retina of Kate's eyes before darkness flooded back … a smaller object like a limp sack lying further down the road…

She managed to quieten the girl's hysteria, and then, telling her to remain where she was, walked slowly forward. She felt deathly sick and her body was trembling uncontrollably as she neared the car. Rain was hissing on red-hot twisted metal and the smell of burnt oil and petrol was sickening now. She passed by the shapeless hulk and a few seconds later was bending over Caroline.

She was lying in a pool of water. With no obvious injuries it seemed at first she was only unconscious. But then, as lightning flashed again, Kate saw the unnatural angle at which her head lay and knew her spine had been broken.

That momentary glimpse of Caroline was one of the things Kate was always to remember. She was lying in the pool like a dead Medusa. Her hair, unloosed by the crash, was floating black around her face. And in the last moment she must have realised her defeat, for death had made a plaster-cast of her fury...

It took Kate all her courage to lay hands on the limp body and drag it to the roadside. Then, grateful for the concealing darkness, she hurried Sarah past towards the main road. With her brain still shocked and Sarah crying hysterically again, she could not convince herself the danger was over at last. Her one compelling thought was to reach Philip, and she urged Sarah on as though Caroline was still hunting for them in the storm and the darkness.

Yet the nightmare was almost over, as Kate realised later that night when she and Philip were back at Whitesands and Sarah safely asleep in her room. Kate had managed to stop a car on the main road and the driver, on hearing her story, had driven them straight round to Philip's offices. He had telephoned the police who had sent men round to Whitesands in an attempt to catch Mrs Treherne. Dry clothes had been found for Sarah and Kate, and after the news had come through that Mrs Treherne had fled Whitesands before the arrival of the police, Philip had brought the two of them back. Sarah had been put to bed after a hot bath and Philip and Kate were now waiting for news in the sitting-room. The storm had long passed although rain could still be heard falling on the terrace outside.

Philip forced another glass of brandy into Kate's hand. 'Drink it, Kate. I want to see some colour come back into your cheeks.'

He filled his own glass and dropped back on the settee alongside her. His dark hair was dishevelled, his white collar torn open at the neck. A residue of amazement was still in his eyes as he stared blindly at the fireplace. 'You know, Kate; I'm still finding all this hard to believe. Caroline, a murderess – it just doesn't seem possible.'

His face, with its marks of shock, made her wonder how much personal pain the news had given him. It made her voice uncertain. 'I can imagine how you feel. I found it difficult enough to believe myself – right until the end.'

He swung round towards her, his voice harsh with disgust. 'But I'm in the legal profession. I'm supposed to be some judge of character, to have an idea when people are lying. And she deceived me completely.'

'You can't blame yourself for that. She was a brilliant actress.'

His pained eyes challenged her. 'You saw through her! Pretty early on, from what you've told me.'

She hadn't bothered to act so well in front of me, Kate thought. In fact, it had been a surprise for her to find another young woman at Whitesands and it had tended to throw her off balance...

She tried to defend him. 'You did guess things. You didn't believe it was chance that took me back to the tower last Saturday. And you were suspicious at my having her binoculars in my pocket out in the garden.'

Her efforts to defend him only added to his self-disgust. 'Right at the end, yes. But those were such obvious things... And I was still miles from the truth.'

You were miles from the truth, Philip, because she had that lovely face and body to blind you with... They couldn't blind me, another woman. She did enchant you, Philip, I know that. But how much were you in love with her...?

'She didn't try to hide the vicious side of her nature from me,' she told him. 'But she was a different person in front of you. And she was your wife's cousin, so I don't see how you can blame yourself for not suspecting her. What reason or motive could you have had?'

Unconvinced he turned restlessly away. 'I wish to God I knew what they did to Elizabeth. If they don't find Mrs Treherne I'll never know.'

'They must find her. She can't have got far away, particularly in this weather.'

He nodded moodily. His reaction seemed to come in waves: after a brief silence she heard his muttered exclamation. 'To think that Sarah's life has been in danger all this time...' There was condemnation in his voice as he swung round on Kate again. 'You should have told me, Kate. After Caroline came into your bedroom with that story about Elizabeth, you ought to have come straight to me and told me everything.'

'I wanted to – terribly. But how could I?' she pleaded. 'All I really had was intuition ... there was no evidence. How could you have believed me if right out of the blue I'd announced she had contrived your wife's death? Even now we don't know how she did it, so what would you have thought then? You'd have thought me crazy... And it would have brought out all the rest about Elizabeth... I couldn't do it to you – can't you see that?'

The resentment faded from his face, to be replaced by an expression she could not interpret. He dropped a hand on hers, pressed it tightly. 'You were thinking of my feelings – I understand that. The trouble is' – and the bleakness in his voice made her wince – 'it might still be true and they used their knowledge of it to drive her to suicide.'

It was possible, she knew, but her love for him would allow him no more pain. 'No; they tricked her in some way. Don't forget the boy, Billy – why were they both so afraid of him? And remember – Mrs Treherne was planted here by Caroline a long time before your wife started going to the summer house. They were behind her actions in some way – I'm certain of it.'

There was a tenderness in his eyes now that made her gaze falter. 'Bless you anyway for the thought, Kate. There'll never be a sweeter-natured person.' He paused, then went on slowly: 'She tried to poison me against you – did you know that?'

Her voice was almost inaudible. 'Yes; I knew.'

'Little things – I see now she was far too clever to overplay her hand. I didn't listen to everything, of course, but here and there I was beginning to think she might be right…' He took her other hand and made her face him. 'I'm ashamed of myself, Kate. Will you forgive me?'

Her throat felt painful. 'There's nothing to forgive. You were never unkind to me.'

'Don't say there's nothing to forgive.

Apart from everything else you saved Sarah's life twice... I'm never going to have another friend like that, Kate.'

Friend... Her mind caught the word and gripped it hard before it could hurt her. In the effort she did not choose her reply as carefully as she would have wished. 'She was very attractive. I'm certain that if I'd been a man I'd have been deceived too.'

His eyebrows drew together as he stared at her. 'What are you saying – that you thought I was in love with her?'

Flushing with embarrassment she tried to turn away but his gripping hands would not allow her to escape the question. 'I thought you were – just a little,' she admitted unsteadily. 'But it was no business of mine.'

His slow headshake was very positive. 'Then you were wrong – that's one of the few things I am sure about. There were times when I found her company attractive – I'll give you that – but love, no...' He released her hands and turned away. When he spoke again his voice had lost its assurance. 'Life's been rather a mix-up since Elizabeth died, Kate. I've never been certain she didn't commit suicide and that's worried me a great deal, particularly as during the last year we seemed somehow to be drifting apart.' As she started to protest he shook his head tersely. 'No; I can't blame all of it on them, unfortunately. It got much worse after Mrs Treherne came, that's true, but a strain was developing before that.' He lit himself a cigarette, exhaled smoke slowly through his nostrils. 'The doctors said it was the illness affecting her mind, but I couldn't help wondering if I was failing her in some way. So it came as a pretty bad shock when she died so mysteriously.'

She yearned to comfort him. 'It was her illness – you must know that, deep inside.'

His voice ran on as if she had not spoken. 'You know how it is after someone close to you has died ... the shock waves keep coming back at all kinds of odd moments until you begin to feel you can't trust your own emotions. That's how I've been these last few months. I couldn't be sure ... I couldn't even decide if I ought to feel that way for another woman so quickly... So after Caroline came and began spreading her poison and you began going out with Dereck, I suppose I just sat back and let things drift...'

Kate could not believe what she was hearing. Astonishment made a marble sculpture of her face as Philip ground out his cigarette and turned to her. She felt his hands on her shoulders.

'Look at me, Kate. It's very important.'

She had no option but to look. The reflection of her white face stared back at her from his eyes.

'What do you think of me, Kate? Please

tell me.'

Again she felt that painful constriction of her throat. 'I don't know what you mean...'

'I think you do. Do you care for me – even a little? Sometimes I've let myself believe that you do. Now it's suddenly very important that I know.'

This time, although she tried hard, she could not speak. Impatience at himself made her voice abrupt. 'I'm doing this very clumsily, I know. All this mumbling and gabbling ... all it really means is that I know now that I'm in love with you.'

She did not hear the rest of his words: they were drowned in the joyous singing that burst out inside her. But a timid part of her that was afraid of dream castles drew back.

'Isn't it too early...? Are you sure, Philip? It might only be gratitude – and I couldn't bear that...'

His eyes were suddenly eager. 'I'm very sure now. But you haven't answered me. Do you care for me, Kate?'

A dam seemed to crumble inside her. 'You know I do,' she sobbed. 'But it all seemed so impossible ... particularly after Caroline came.'

His arms closed around her, drew her to him. All her pent-up emotions from violence and fear seemed to be released in that long kiss, leaving her weak and trembling.

'Why wasn't I sure before?' he murmured,

lips buried in her hair. 'Why was I such a blind fool?'

'How could you be sure?' she sobbed. 'First there was your grief for Elizabeth, and then there was Caroline and her lies... How could either of us be sure of anything?'

'I'm very sure now, my darling,' he said, quietly, kissing her again. 'Surer than I've been of anything in my life.'

At that moment the telephone in the hall rang. Feeling him stiffen Kate drew back. 'It's probably the police. They might have caught Mrs Treherne.'

He nodded and rose. Thinking he might prefer to be alone if there were news of how Elizabeth had died Kate pressed his hand. 'I'll wait in here while you answer it.'

He returned ten minutes later. There was a bleak, shocked expression in his eyes that made her jump up in alarm.

'What is it, darling? Have they caught her?'

He nodded. Anxiously she led him to the settee and lit him a cigarette. He attempted a smile and her breath caught at the strain in it.

'What's happened, darling? Please tell me if you can.'

He drew deeply on the cigarette. 'They caught Mrs Treherne in Okehampton; she'd got a lift in a lorry as far as that. She's made a full confession at headquarters.'

It was about Elizabeth then... Kate's breath

felt tight in her chest as she waited. For what seemed an endless time Philip sat staring blindly ahead as if seeing some nightmare vision in his mind. Then he partially recovered and turned to her.

'You were right in your suspicions of Caroline – she was behind all that happened. Apparently the idea came to her during one of her earlier visits: in one of them she found out Elizabeth was ill and in another she noticed how it was making her suspicious. So she decided to use the illness as a means of destroying her. She planted Mrs Treherne here – apparently it wasn't the first time the two of them had worked together – and the unholy work on Elizabeth began...' His voice caught; he recovered immediately, pretending he had only paused to inhale on is cigarette, but she was not deceived. Her arms went out to him.

'What is it, darling? What did they do to her?'

For a moment he allowed her to draw his dishevelled head against her shoulder. Gazing down, seeing the silver strands running through the thick black hair of his temples, she felt a sympathy and love that was almost too much to bear. 'Don't talk about it now if it hurts too much,' she whispered. 'Wait until later.'

He shook his head and drew back. 'No; I'd rather tell you now. Mrs Treherne's first task was to win Elizabeth's confidence. Caroline told her to take her time; she had to be intimate enough to talk about me to Elizabeth before the filthy business could start.'

'You!' Kate exclaimed.

He nodded. 'Yes. That story Caroline gave you to explain their fear of Billy was brilliantly clever – almost every fact in it was true except the reason Elizabeth kept going to the summer house.' His eyes, swollen with pain and bitterness, lifted to her face. 'She wasn't having any affair there, Kate. I was the one having the affair – that was why she kept going there on the nights I was working late.'

Kate's head was reeling. 'I don't understand.'

'It's simple enough. On Caroline's instructions Mrs Treherne planted the suspicion in Elizabeth's mind that I was meeting a woman in the summer house on the nights I was supposed to be at the office. The idea – at least this is what Mrs Treherne swears Caroline told her – was to turn Elizabeth against me so she would sue for divorce. But I don't believe that, and neither does Mrs Treherne now...'

He took a glass of brandy and drank deeply. Kate waited, muscles tensed with shock, as he turned back to her.

'Mrs Treherne's job was to plant small incriminating things in the summer house –

things sufficient to keep Elizabeth's suspicions at fever pitch without giving her any certain proof. It was sadism really – calculated to destroy an unbalanced mind. This went on in the month before Christmas. And then Caroline let Mrs Treherne know the time had come to finish the business. She was coming herself over Christmas to handle it. She gave Mrs Treherne no details – only that she was going to plant certain evidence herself that would convince Elizabeth beyond doubt of my infidelity.'

The blonde woman coming to the summer house with Mrs Treherne, Kate thought... Billy seeing them and hiding behind the hedge... How brilliantly Caroline had covered up when Billy had returned to Whitesands, using every fact that had occurred and yet fitting them to make an entirely new pattern... She listened breathlessly to Philip's tight, bitter voice.

'She came in secrecy and hid in the summer house. Then she instructed Mrs Treherne to tell Elizabeth later that night that she had seen a woman, my mistress, making across the cliffs. She couldn't have picked a more opportune time: Mrs Treherne had already found out earlier that I had to go over to Exeter, Elizabeth was suffering from one of her fevers, and there was a half-gale blowing that night...'

As though it were a film in her mind Kate

could see the climax of the plot unfolding. Elizabeth, restless with fever in her bed, her mind unbalanced and suspicious, learning from Mrs Treherne that at last she had a chance of exposing her husband's mistress... The fierce gale shuddering the windows of Whitesands... Mrs Treherne making a pretence of holding Elizabeth back and then watching with satisfaction as the frail, feverish woman started out over the black cliffs... But at that point the screen in her mind went dark. What had happened out there, high over the sea, in the fierce gale and the rain?

Philip saw the unspoken question in her eyes and shook his head. 'No; Mrs Treherne doesn't know for certain what happened – Caroline told her later that Elizabeth never reached the summer house and so must either have had an accident or committed suicide. But Mrs Treherne admits she believes Caroline murdered her. She'd never bargained getting herself mixed up in a murder and it's been preying on her mind ever since.'

'It could have been an accident,' Kate said in an effort to ease his pain. 'You say yourself the wind was very fierce that night.'

'No, or why should Caroline have tried to kill Sarah? She wasn't the type to panic – she must have had a good reason, before trying something as desperate as that. No; I have to face it, Kate – she killed Elizabeth.' His brows furrowed heavily in an effort to understand his emotions. 'At the moment I can't think which seems worse – that or suicide…' Then his voice caught again and he turned sharply away. 'One thing I do know – I do wish I'd had some idea what was going on in Elizabeth's mind before it happened…'

This, she knew, was one of the deepest wounds that had been inflicted on him tonight – the knowledge that his wife had died believing him unfaithful and unloving. She took one of his hands and held it to her face. 'She'll know the truth now,' she whispered. 'She might even have known it before she died.'

Emotion made his hand tighten. She felt his recovery in its gradual slackening. 'You wouldn't believe a woman could be such a devil, would you?' he said slowly. Then he turned fully towards her, his face twisted in a parody of a smile. 'It's a bit ironical, isn't it, that the children, particularly Sarah, should have an instinctive fear of Mrs Treherne and yet apparently liked Caroline.'

Kate frowned. 'I've often wondered that myself. But now I think the reason is that there was good in Mrs Treherne as well as bad. I believe her if she says she didn't know Caroline was going to murder Elizabeth: she certainly opposed Caroline when she discovered her intentions against Sarah. What I'm trying to say is that I think it was the better side of her nature that made her worse side the more obvious.'

'I know what you mean. She was human: she had an inner conflict, probably it was the reason for her sullenness. But Caroline' – his voice was infinitely bitter – 'she hadn't any such problems to worry her.'

Kate was thinking of the lamia of her nightmare. 'Her evil was so undiluted she could enchant with it...' As she spoke she was back on the road, with the car and its brilliant headlights screaming down on her. His arms went round her as she shuddered.

'What is it, darling?'

'I could see her car again... It was so close, Philip...'

His face was pale again. 'I don't know how you escaped. The banks are almost vertical at that point.'

Her voice was muffled by his jacket. 'It was the sudden downpour of rain that blinded her ... I saw her lose control at the last moment...' She pressed her face harder into his shoulder. 'Oh, God; she frightened me, Philip. I always thought everyone was a mixture of good and bad... But she – I hope I never meet anyone like her again.'

'You won't, my darling. It's all over now. After a night's sleep things will seem very different.'

She shivered. Tomorrow, she knew, he would help her to forget. But tonight Caroline was still very close... 'No; I don't want to sleep – I couldn't... Please stay down here with me, Philip. It's not long to morning...'

He kissed her gently. 'I'll stay with you, darling. For always, if you'll have me.'

And so, in each other's arms, they waited for the dawn that was to bring a new day and a new life to them both.

The publishers hope that this book has given you enjoyable reading. Large Print Books are especially designed to be as easy to see and hold as possible. If you wish a complete list of our books please ask at your local library or write directly to:

Dales Large Print Books
Magna House, Long Preston,
Skipton, North Yorkshire.
BD23 4ND

This Large Print Book, for people
who cannot read normal print,
is published under the auspices of

THE ULVERSCROFT FOUNDATION